Prize Fighter

Rydon Tyme: The Life of the Eye

3 of 5

Ali Muhammad

Prize Fighter is a fictitious story inspired by historic events, imaginative thoughts, and real life experiences of the Author.

Published by Leaders of Tomorrow, Today LLC
PO Box 470 Oshtemo, MI 49077
First Edition

ISBN- 978-1-7356687-3-4

Editor: M. Araujo, E. Ivy
Cover Illustrator: Brian Nickson
Story Illustrator: Aires Melo
Royal Comics | Sneak Peek Illustrator: Michael Briggs
Graphic Designer: LOTT Art Department

Dedication

This book is dedicated to those who inspire me up close: The strongest person I know, my Mother. My role model and Father, my first mentors, my big brother and big sister.

I also dedicate this book to my grandparents, aunts, uncles, cousins, my niece, nephew, and fiancée.

My friends, family friends, and those who inspire me from afar: Athletes, entertainers, scholars, world leaders, etc. Your journeys fueled my passions which gave me the stamina to pursue my dreams.

Visit www.LOTT48203.com for books, blogs, careers, competitions, interviews, Hear Me Out: Unscripted, magazines, photo albums, press conferences, scholarship information, LOTT Sportswear, official Prize Fighter book trailers, and more.

CONTENTS

"MAKE A SPLASH IN THE WORLD"

www.LOTT48203.com

Briefly escaping the rigors of his daily operations through the underwater Detroit-Windsor Tunnel, Detective Rydon Tyme chanced his luck on a good ole game of Table Dice. Rydon and his bride, Gabriella, never hesitated to wave farewell to Lady Liberty when things got too tough to bear. Ultimately, they controlled their own happiness.

"In what denomination would you like your chips, sir?" the cashier asked.

"Two hundred in fives, the rest in fifties," Rydon replied.

"Eight hundred in fifty-dollar chips and two hundred in five-dollar chips."

"Keep it down. That's my business, not everyone in line behind me," Rydon scolded.

"My apologies, Mr. Tyme. It's standard protocol. Good luck." The man waved farewell.

Growing up during an era of constant battles for equality, Rydon became more and more impulsively outspoken. Exposed to many of life's harshest realities associated in his line of work, his thirties brought a new standard of expectations from everyone around him.

"Here, baby, take these. Mirror what I do, and I'll make you a rich woman," Rydon said, splitting the chips in half.

"And what if I don't want to?" Gabriella smirked.

"Then I can say, *I told you* later on as I collect my money."

"Whatever you say, man. We'll see."

Approaching the table as if it were the batter's box, Rydon confidently placed his money on the table. Scoping his environment and studying the scene, he placed more bets on the shooter.

"Remember, play what I play," he whispered.

"The point is nine," the gamesman shouted.

Reaching across the table, Rydon placed fifty-dollar side bets for numbers six, eight, and ten.

"And the number is eleven, yo!"

"I'll take that," Gabriella said, collecting her earnings.

"Look at you. Maybe you do know a thing or two about shooting dice after all."

"Yo! Eleven again," the gamesman said after another roll.

"And maybe you should have bet with me instead." Gabriella smiled, racking up her earnings.

"Nobody bets on four and five, Gabby," Rydon warned, as Gabriella placed additional side bets. "But you are getting lucky with that eleven." He continued to study the table.

In the midst of a friendly competition between spouses, Gabriella switched her fifty-dollar chip to a spot on the table designated for one time rolls.

"Baby, you know if this guy doesn't roll a three, you lose right?" Rydon said.

"Well, I suggest you put your money on three then, Ry," she replied, waiting on the gamesman's call.

"Two and one makes three," the gamesman bellowed, pointing at the table game.

"I'm going to close my mouth. I see you have this under control," Rydon replied, wearing a look of confusion as the gamesman continued.

Deuce deuce is a happy 4!

5!

Yo, lucky number 11!

And there is the missing number 9 that started it all.

Gabriella's chips increased rapidly while Rydon's showed minimal growth. Lady Luck stood next to him in the flesh as he stared on in disbelief.

"Who are you?" Rydon asked, seeing Gabriella in a new light because of her pleasant surprises.

"I told you to bet on big mama, maybe you should start listening more," Gabriella smiled.

"I guess I should," Rydon chuckled, slapping his forehead.

"Excuse me, Mr. Tyme? There is a call for you," one of the casino attendants who suddenly joined the table said.

Puzzled, Rydon's head filled with questions. "Are you talking to me?" he asked.

"Well, that depends, are you Mr. Rydon Tyme?"

"Who's asking?"

"He wouldn't give us a name, but said you'd know who he is," the attendant replied.

"This is a joke, right?"

"Not at all, sir. He said to tell you, *life or liberty* if you didn't believe me."

Life or Liberty was a phrase turned organization Rydon and friends created one day in the playing fields, long ago. They all took an oath to protect each other's life and liberty if it was within means.

During the summer of 1938, gangs of teens from other neighborhoods were always causing havoc on Rydon's street corner. They stole bikes, egged houses, toilet papered trees and homes, roughing up anyone who tried to stop them.

Rydon and his friends were able to avoid the gang for most of the summer until one of his closest friends became the mob's latest victim. Rydon assembled a team of ten other boys from his neighborhood and the gym

where he boxed. Outnumbered two to one, they trusted their lives and liberty in each other's hands.

Their only objective was to protect their family, friends, and community from invasion. After their confrontation with the savages, they ran them out of town, never to be seen again.

"How did he know I was here?" Rydon wondered.

"He said they all know you're here and to quote, *Stop asking so many questions and come to the phone. I don't have much time.* Here, sir. I wrote it down," the man replied, handing Rydon a message slip.

"Keep doing what you're doing, baby. I'll be right back," Rydon said, kissing Gabriella's blushed cheeks.

Walking through the casino as if he was running late to a championship bout, Rydon entered the Guest Services office ready for answers.

"Hello! Who's this?" Rydon exclaimed. "It can only be one out of ten people."

"Don't say my name, brother," a voice calmly spoke on the other end of the phone.

"Good to hear from you, it's been a long time. People been asking about you."

"Let them ask. I don't have much time, but I need a meeting at the spot. This Friday, five minutes to six."

"You think we can round everyone up so close to the holiday? Unless you have a private jet, I don't know about that," Rydon stated.

"You're a funny guy. I don't need to meet with everyone, just you."

"Everything alright your way?" Rydon asked, hoping for good news.

"I'll tell you everything you want to know. Friday, at what time?"

"I'll be there at five minutes to six. You just make sure you're on time."

"Even when I'm late, I'm on time."

Click

Exiting the office equally as confused as he entered, Rydon blazed through the casino lobby as a man on a mission. Cheers bouncing off the tables in every direction, helped him get in the zone. Placing two, fifty-dollar chips on point number five, he was back in the game.

"Is that your wife with the dice?" a stranger inquired.

"Yes, why you asking?" Rydon replied, short on patience.

"No disrespect, sir, I just wanted to say thanks. I won four hundred, ninety-five dollars betting on her today. I got laid off a little over a year ago and my savings account has been low for months now. That's what brought me across the bridge.

"I came for the open interviews working in the kitchen or on table games. They said they would call me. When I was on my way out, I stopped at the fountains for a little peace of mind and found a five-dollar chip.

"I know you're probably wondering why I'm telling you all of this. Just this afternoon, those interviews were my only hope to make some money. I'm a month behind on my rent and spent my last coming here, prepared to walk back to the States.

"I took that five-dollar chip from the fountains as a sign from the universe to take more risks in my life. One thing I don't do, is ignore signs from the universe. So, I gathered myself, rubbed my head for good luck, and got on the table," the man shrugged, fixing his suit. Unable to hide his smile.

"Usually, I only bet on myself, so I was holding onto my chip until the dice came my way. Then I saw your wife win on the solo roll three and again with the four and five. I would've been plain ole stubborn to bet against Lady Luck today.

"I turned a five-dollar chip into five hundred dollars, just by betting when she did. Now I can lease me one of those fancy Pentagon trucks for my tools. Pay my rent up and go into business for myself. If you ever need any plumbing or electric work, look me up. Crispus Forten. It's on the house.

Good luck and have a good one, sir," Crispus said, grinning as he left the table.

Speechless to the confessions of a random stranger, Rydon looked at his wife and surveyed the table as always before placing more bets. Only this time, things had drastically changed.

"What did I miss?" he asked the crowd.

"Hold your tongue, young man. Lady Luck has the dice," an older gentleman said from his seat, marveling at the situation with a captivated smile on his face.

Rydon noticed all eyes were fixed on the most beautiful woman he'd ever seen. The others may have been stunned by her radiant skin, but mostly they were waiting to see what she would roll next.

Double three makes six.

"Yes!"

Turning to the sound of voices, he saw a middle aged woman and others around the table collect over five hundred dollars in chips. As the dealer slid the dice to Gabriella, she seemed uncertain for the first time.

Without any further thought, she withdrew her chips from the table, leaving only her locked bets before releasing the dice from her hands.

Five and a one, six again

"There it is," one man shouted.

Four and one is a mighty five!

"Thanks, baby." Rydon grinned.

And five plus two makes seven. Game over.

The table applauded as Gabriella collected her earnings before being escorted to the chip exchange desk.

"How would you like your money, ma'am?"

"Large bills, please," she requested.

"Very well, congratulations and please come again."

Smiling as they exited toward the elevators in the lobby, "Told ya," was all she had to say, leaving Rydon in complete disarray. His life changed so much in less than an hour. He didn't know where to start.

Windsor, Ontario
Casino 21 Palace Suites, Room 1914
11:11:pm Eastern Standard Time
1958 December 31, Wednesday

"You won. Even though I didn't get to play much, you definitely won. Hands down, all hail the Queen!" Rydon announced, barging into the penthouse suite.

"You are so dramatic. You should have seen it, baby. It was magical. I couldn't miss out there. After you left, I made a couple side bets and started making money betting on other shooters.

"When the dice came to me, I kept rolling fives, nines, and double fives. The gamesman called them puppy paws, because the dots on the dice kind of look like puppy paws if you tilt your head and squint your eyes a little. It was so cute."

"The dice were cute, and I'm the dramatic one?" Rydon laughed. "I'm listening."

"You better be listening with those great big ol' ears on the side of your head." Gabriella giggled.

Rydon naturally reached for his offside earlobe at Gabriella's remarks.

"I'm sorry, Ry. Come here. You know I love your ears. They're so soft and rubby."

"Rubby?"

"Mmm hmm. You know, fun to rub and play with," she said, caressing him.

"My ears are soft and fun to play with? You crack me up," he said, chuckling. "Enough about my listeners, I want to hear the rest of your story."

"Ok, so... I started seeing people win more money off of me than I was. I didn't really know what I was doing. I was just betting on numbers that popped in my head before I shot the dice. Then I started doubling the amount of chips the guy next to the gamesman bet."

"That was your strategy? That guy was playing with five-hundred-dollar chips."

"I know..."

"Gab, how much did you win?" Rydon asked, blown away by it all.

"Ten thousand, well... nine thousand, five hundred," she answered, blushing through her freckles.

"You turned five hundred dollars into twenty times that, in thirty minutes? Unbelievable... do you know how long it takes me to make ten thousand dollars?"

"No."

"Me either. Not off the top of my head but I'm sure it's much longer than thirty minutes. What made you bet so much? I didn't know you had it in you," Rydon said, chuckling.

"I told you, baby, it felt magical. But I knew when to quit. I almost put it all back on the table before we left. Just to see what would happen. And that's when I rolled the seven."

"You lost after I came back. Had I stayed away, you'd be a millionaire by now," Rydon said, snapping his fingers.

"Child, please. That had nothing to do with you. It was time to go. If I kept playing, I would've lost eventually. The house always wins."

"Touché."

"Who was that on the phone, the president? I've never seen you move so fast in silk before," she joked with the smooth operator.

"No, it wasn't the president, Gabby. It was Big Jo. I haven't heard from him in years," Rydon replied, laughing.

"How is he and why did he call you at the casino?"

"I don't know. He said he wants to meet with me on Friday about something."

10

"Be careful, Ry. You know how you get when you and Jo are around each other."

"What's that supposed to mean? How do I get?"

"Like him, loud and angry at the world."

"Baby, he's changed. Besides, I'm like that all the time. You just keep me steady. So, you never see that side of me until he's around. Big Jo wasn't loud until he met me by the way. They used to call him Big Teddy. He's getting back to his ways," Rydon said, shrugging.

"Like a teddy bear?" Gabriella asked, snickering. "Aww."

"I can't make this stuff up," he said, chuckling as he gathered his things.

"You are really something else. It's almost midnight, Ry, are you ready?"

"I am and look who's under the mistletoe," Rydon said, holding a holiday surprise above her head.

"Baby, if you keep it up, we'll miss the Desires," she warned.

"What time do they hit the stage?"

"In less than an hour and I still have to finish getting dressed," she answered back.

"Good thing the auditorium is downstairs."

Entering the elevator ten minutes before showtime, Gabriella straightened her dress, fixing pieces of wayward hazel streaked tresses that had fallen out of place. Leaning against the man of her dreams, she snuggled under him until reaching the ground level of the Grand Auditorium.

"I told you we'd make it on time," Rydon assured her.

Dressed in a black-on-black tuxedo with a Windsor knotted black tie to match his location. Rydon perfectly complemented Gabriella's breathtaking red gown. Its silky, rippled layers stacked atop her body's curves in neatly arranged piles.

The dress was one of a kind, designed exclusively for her by THE Rosa Louverture. All eyes were on Mr. and Mrs. Tyme the moment they walked in. It wouldn't be right if one half of the dynamic duo didn't particularly care for the extra attention.

"What are these people staring at? Do I have something in my nose?" Rydon wondered, wiping his face.

"No, Ry, they're looking at us. We look good, baby, own it."

"Well, I don't like it," he replied with a wrinkle between his eyebrows.

Taking their seats front row center, all of the lights in the building shut off as the doors to the auditorium were closed shut.

Being overly aware due to events of his past, Rydon stayed alert assuming someone was always lurking in the shadows. "Baby, relax. It's part of the show. No one knows we're here," Gabriella reminded him.

Over the last thirty-six months, Detective Rydon Tyme worked double time cleaning the streets of Detroit and its Brother City, Highland Park. On top of it all, he prosecuted his own cases. Free time had become a foreign commodity that he missed greatly.

On a quest for the truth, every book he read brought him a step closer to discovering the answers he sought. His thirties eliminated all patience for cover ups, lies, excuses, and injustice.

Mothers across the Brother Cities wrote letters by the sack load, hoping he'd represent their sons who were lost in the thug life. It wasn't uncommon for Detective Tyme to receive blank checks in the mail for his services. He wanted to save them all, but it just wasn't enough hours in a day.

His first private investigation firm was established on the eve of his thirtieth birthday. He and four other detectives left the police force to trial and sentence over a dozen crooked law enforcement officers. The only problem was the feathers he ruffled in the process.

Rydon was sworn into secrecy when he vowed to protect and serve the people of the Great Lake State of Michigan. Police officers were his closest allies but those who were corrupt stood in his way of bringing peace to the streets. They had become part of the problem.

Surprisingly, most the people he busted were willing and ready to change. After rehabilitation, officers were retrained at Right On Time Enterprises in downtown Highland Park.

Officers would then be reeducated on ethics, morals, and the effects tyranny had on the oppressed. The irony of it all, the instructors of the courses were the same felons Rydon represented or imprisoned throughout his career.

Those yet to be seized, caused Rydon to constantly stare over his shoulder, incorporating his Lethal Lenses into his daily attire. "I'm fine, sweetheart. The night vision kicks in automatically. Here comes Cliff."

"Hello, everyone and thank you for coming out. I'm Clifton Adams, one fifth of the Desires," Clifton said, introducing himself to the crowd as the spotlights activated.

"Thank you, thank you. Thank you very much. I hope no one dropped their nachos when we hit the lights but as you all know, we are the original Show Stoppers and we had to get this party started right. Are you all ready to have some fun tonight?"

"Yea," the audience replied.

"That was weak. Bishop, take the microphone over there and see if the right side is ready to boogie because the left side is still sleeping. It might be past their bedtime. It is almost midnight and all."

"We both know the right side is ready, I don't even have to ask. But I guess I'll do it anyway. Right side, are you all ready to get down!?"

The Desires had a strong international following, especially in neighboring Windsor. Whenever they were on tour, it was always the last stop before returning to Detroit, closing out at the Pyramid in front of the hometown fans.

"Left side did you hear that? I know you did. I think they heard that over in Detroit. Left side, we're going to let them have round one. So that means we have to come out strong for round two. Left side, open the envelopes strapped under your chairs and read it when I count to three.

1.... 2.... 3!"

HAPPY NEW YEAR!

The crowd roared with excitement. No two shows were ever alike with the Desires. Anything could happen at any given moment. Their stage presence was second to none, leaving people in awe with stories to tell for weeks on end.

"We have a great show planned for you all tonight, and the fellas came up with a melody for the ladies in the house to kick things off. Go ahead, fellas!"

You are sooooo beautiful:
The way your hair blows with the wind.

You are sooooo beautiful:
I love your eyes and glowing skin.

You are sooooo beautiful:
You're so fine. Would you please, be mine?

Be Mine, Be Mine

Would you please, be mine?

Be Mine, Be Mine

The background singers echoed in perfect harmony, dancing across the stage.

The Desires smoothly transitioned into the first set of the show, performing their number one hit single on the Soul Music Charts, *Be Mine*.

Their nearest and dearest fans reacted in volumes to the sultry serenade.

"Aww," the ladies in the crowd said in unison, unexpectedly.

"I love you!!" a woman shouted from the back.

"And we love you back. Hit it, fellas!" Clifton shouted, pointing at the band.

Highland Park, Michigan
Paradise Condominiums, Manchester Street
5:30PM Eastern Standard Time
1959 January 2, Friday

"What are you doing home, big head? I thought you were meeting up with Jo today?"

"I am, it's just down the street. We'll be at Rocket Park. If anything happens to me, the key I gave you a long time ago goes to the safe in my storage unit," Rydon said, closing the front door behind him, holding a stack of mail.

"Ry, you know I hate it when you talk like this. If you don't feel safe, maybe you should take some time off," Gabriella suggested, frowning, as she slumped on the front room couch.

"I'll always be alright, Gabby, even when I'm not. But Jo really does bring trouble with him on accident sometimes. I actually came home to tell you about a guy you really helped out the other day."

"What did I do?" she asked, springing up from her seat with a puzzled look on her face.

"You gave a man his big break and now, he's an entrepreneur. He told me you helped him win five hundred, well..." he added mockingly. "Four hundred, ninety-five dollars on the tables at the casino. But this is where it gets wild.

"The man said to look him up for electric and plumbing work if we ever needed it. Now, what are the odds of the power going out at the office today? I called him to do the work for us and he already has a truck and two men working for him. You make people better and you don't even know it."

"Wow. I don't know what to say," Gabriella replied in surprise.

"That was only two days ago. I guess it really does take money to make money. I'd bet my last dollar that there's people all over the world with great ideas without money or resources to do anything about it," Rydon said, still thumbing through the mail.

"I've been thinking about what I was going to do with all that money. We could set up an organization like that to help out more folks. Put an ad in Sunday's paper and we're good to go."

"You're going to use all that money on startup costs?" Rydon replied.

"I didn't say that, Beany. I said *we* as in the both of us. I'll put up twenty-five hundred. I know you can match it. I've seen your bankbook.

"I'm buying a pink Pentagon Pleasure this weekend. They're so small and sporty. Then, I'll do a little shopping and save the rest. I already bought you a little something too, I'll show you when you get home. So, hurry back."

"I'll be back quicker than a hare in the woods, racing a tortoise *without* a nap. You ever think of how that story would have ended if the hare never napped? If he lapped the tortoise like he should have, what would have been the moral of the story? It's not sweet in these streets, that's what!" he said, opening the front door of the condominium.

"I cannot believe you just ruined one of my favorite childhood stories. Thanks a lot, Ry. Just get out, man!" she said, laughing as she shoved Rydon out with a kiss goodbye.

"I love you," he laughed.

"I love you too, be safe."

Highland Park, Michigan
Rocket Park
5:50PM Eastern Standard Time
1959 January 2, Friday

Leaving his penthouse condominium, dressed in fatigues, black jeans and boots. Rydon took Manchester to John R, turning east on Gerald Street. He reached Rocket Park with five seconds to spare.

Climbing out of his 1958 Pentagon Sunset, Rydon pulled the door down as he locked the shell to his capsuled-shaped sports car. With his car matching the greens in his shirt, Jo had to make a scene. "Who said street hustlas were the only ones making money in the city?" he said, clapping his hands.

"Big Jo, long time no nothing. What's going on, brother? How did you find me in a casino? You had me paranoid for the rest of the trip," Rydon stated, shaking hands with his old friend.

"I didn't mean to ruin your vacation, brother. But you and Gabriella have been going across the water for New Year's Eve every year since you got married. The hard part was describing you to the square who answered the phone. Tyme, I'm in a jam. A big time jam, my man."

"That's why I'm here, brother. What's on your mind?" Rydon asked, looking upwards to make eye contact.

"My ex-girlfriend is coming after me."

"Margret? I told you to do right by her. I don't know what you're running from. Love is a beautiful thing," Rydon said, joking.

"No, not Margo, ear flaps," Jo snapped back, getting to the point. "I'm talking about Miss Karma. My past is coming back to haunt me."

"Is it the haircut, or because I cut the sideburns? Why does everyone keep talking about my ears all of a sudden? Everybody gets one and that's yours," Rydon said, holding his earlobe, pointing up at Jo.

"But you still haven't said much. You've done a lot of things that can catch up to you. Talk to me, Big Jo," Rydon countered, looking for answers.

Rydon Tyme and Jo Rivers were mirror images of each other, living opposite lifestyles. Both men were recognized by the public as being the best at what they did for a living. Rydon earned his stripes working alongside Detroit and Highland Park's Finest. They were his employers. Running his own independent practice, Rydon's caseload came directly from the Chief of Police in both cities.

Jo, on the other hand, chose a completely different lifestyle. Standing beside each other, they look to be in the same tax bracket. Legally, on paper, one of the two has yet to report his income or cash a paycheck.

"This goes back to the late forties, early fifties. Remember when I used to run numbers for Henton over on Woodward Ave?"

"He lived down the street from me. That was right after I graduated from Cal Midwest," Rydon recalled.

"Bingo! Around the time you helped bring the Levi family together. You weren't even twenty, were you?"

"I was sixteen years old," Rydon answered, shaking his head in disbelief.

"Now you see why I called you, this is your calling, Don. You're here to save knuckle heads like me. Must be tough," Jo said, laughing as he slapped Rydon's back with a heavy hand.

"Sometimes I don't want to get out of bed, bro. But this is the life I chose," Rydon admitted with a shrug.

"It's the life that chose you, brother. You're the only one who can get it done."

"I appreciate that, Jo. I really do," Rydon said, pounding fists as Jo finished his story.

"One day, we were at a house on Davison with two sacks. One was the money and the other had the losing numbers. We got sloppy during daylight hours and two patrollers saw us take them out of the trunk when they were driving down the street.

"Running numbers in the 1940s was an everyday thing, so they knew what was going on. They busted us and took our bags, but they didn't take us in."

"Uh-oh," Rydon paused, seeing where the story was headed.

"Yea, *uh-oh* is right. I memorized their badge numbers and went to the police station and just like I thought, they never turned in the money. That's when I filed a complaint.

"After that, they were watching us at the house off of Brush. We got sloppy and they busted us, again. Except this time, they took the money and threatened us not to say nothing about it.

"Well, the type of person that I am, I did the opposite. I went to the police station that day and made another report. Only this time, they called the officers to the station. They opened the trunk to the squad car and there were my bags. They took pictures of what was in the bags and gave them back to me. In exchange, I agreed not to go to the newspaper like I said I would."

As tensions from the Civil Rights War made its way up north, police departments across the city received astronomically high volumes of complaints.

The people didn't stop at the phones. Petitions were signed. Protests were staged at City Hall Meetings. Citizens did whatever it took to get the police department to take accountability for the bad apples that spoiled their bunch.

Citizens' efforts created a new city law mandating an open investigation on police officers, after every fifth complaint. Chief Dean Carter Jibril didn't view himself as a heavy bag and only agreed to investigate his squad under his own terms.

His first request was for the people to stop provoking officers to become reactionaries and to behave as normal law-abiding citizens. His second demand was to recognize standout officers by sending letters and stories to the Detroit Press Report and Highland Park Sun newspapers.

Thirdly, the first day of every April was to be coined as Officer's Day, where the people would police themselves, acting with integrity for twenty-four straight hours. With officers supervising the situation nearby.

The Self Police Act went into effect April 1, 1957. A day designated for pranks, laughs, and giggles was the beginning of something special throughout Wayne County.

"The officer was suspended for a couple weeks, paid leave. Ever since, Officer Conner has been after me. We closed down the Brush house for a while. About a year later, we reopened it for business, and they kicked in the door waving the forty-fours. I did three years in the penitentiary on my first offense for racketeering, which still doesn't add up to me."

"That was the reason I went to law school. You should've gotten probation, but definitely not more than a year without any priors," Rydon said.

"That's why I called you. After I was released, I couldn't find a job. No one wants to hire a felon. After living on my mother's couch for two years, I applied at Highland Park City College and ran into Henton on campus.

"He told me he used the money from running numbers to pay for his classes. He was finishing up his Associates in Accounting before transferring to Michigan International University at the Buena Vista Campus in Kalamazoo."

"I didn't know either of you went to college. You learn something new every day," Rydon said as he nodded.

"I didn't stay long. But he graduated with a Bachelor's degree in Mathematics. Now he owns a couple of soul food spots in Kalamazoo. Right on Stadium Drive and another one on the corner of Drake and KL" Jo said.

"Good for him. I'm glad he got out the game before it was too late."

"That's why we're here, Don. I can't say anything else to protect you. What you don't know can't hurt me if you're ever asked to testify on my behalf in court. All you'll be able to say are the great things I'm going to bring your way, Champ."

"I was with you in the beginning, but you lost me at *Champ*," Rydon said, laughing.

"Well, Don, I need a character witness. Marcel is in charge at the gym now, but his fighters have a long way to go to do what I need done."

"Speak English, Jo," Rydon replied.

"Don, I need you to fight for me. Marcel can make you a champion."

"Why would he do that?" Rydon chuckled, still confused from it all.

"Life or Liberty, he's honoring his word," Jo answered.

"How does this all relate, Jo? I don't get it."

"The courts need to see that I've been making money, legally. Promotions is my specialty. I would've taken up Marketing sooner, but I pursued a different career."

"So, why do you need me?"

"You're the best fighter I know who's still in shape. The ones who are fit don't have your hand and foot speed. Not to mention your quickness on defense."

"I'm not in boxing shape. I'm a healthy two-fifteen right now. What about Marcel?" Rydon bounced back.

"Why would the heavyweight champion come out of retirement to work with an unknown promoter? But him helping a longtime friend is much more believable. I need a stranger to the boxing world. Everybody loves the underdog.

"With me promoting your fights, I can make us both millionaires. The Pyramid fits one hundred fifty-five thousand. You'll headline the fight of the century in six to eighteen months.

"I can make you a star. I know I've never promoted a fight, but you know I can get it done. I can sell a smile to a proud mom and dad, happy to sad. Last week, I sold a bark to a dog. I'm so smooth with words I can translate the ribbit of a frog."

"As cool as you just made all of that sound, I don't want to be a star, Jo," Rydon said with certainty.

"And I don't want to go back to jail, Don. Especially for something that happened so long ago. Again, I can't tell you too much, but trust me on this one," Jo replied.

Hanging his head, the words *Life or Liberty* rang through his eardrum. "Gabby was telling me earlier that I should take a break. But a year and a half is a long time to be off the job."

"Your staff can handle it. You trained them for times like this."

"That's not why I trained them at all, but I get your point. When do I start?" Rydon asked, stretching his arms and neck before shadowboxing. "Mr. Promoter Man, sir!" Rydon saluted.

"I appreciate it, brother! I'll see you at the gym. Monday morning at five minutes to six."

"That's too early."

"The early birds win championships."

"What am I supposed to tell Gabby?"

"Tell her *the early birds win championships.*"

Highland Park, Michigan
15500 Woodward Avenue
5:55AM Eastern Standard Time
1959 January 5, Monday

"You run like a cop. You've been detective so long you lost your swagger. Loosen up, Champ!"

"I run like a cop? That's a good thing, Marcel. Try finding one woman who says, I don't look like the one, when I'm running and my badge flies through the wind," Rydon darted back, jogging next to Jo's pickup truck.

Marcel sat in the back, throwing watermelons at Rydon that were dodged or punched through. Tosses came at various speeds, up and down Woodward Avenue.

"Champions don't have to run to impress the ladies. We just hold the belt and pose for the camera. The One, I like it. That's your new name for now, Champ," Marcel yelled, throwing a watermelon at Rydon's torso.

Marcel was the livewire of the crew. He and Rydon brought out the best in each other. During their days training at The Bag as amateur boxers, they were both top ten juniors in their weight classes.

The Bag was a historic, Highland Park recreation center. Established in 1815 by four men: Toussaint Freeman, Wallace Goodson, Roy Shabazz and Eli Tyme. The Bag groomed some of the greatest boxers in the history of the sport.

Flash Shabazz, Icy Isa, Raphael Ruh, Bernard 'Blackout' Beason and The Masterful Marcel Riaz represented generations of champions who trained at The Bag. Boxers signed contracts as fighters that expired well beyond their days inside the four corners.

After retirement, fighters turned into recruiters in search of the next big thing to fill their void. Rydon veered away from the Professional Boxing Association once in the past, in favor of a track and field scholarship at California Midwest University.

In the meantime, five of his Life or Liberty brothers went on to become lightweight, welterweight, middleweight, super middleweight, and heavyweight champions of the world. "Alright, Champ, jump rope for ten minutes, hit the bag for ten minutes.

"Lift five sets of ten. We're working with one twenty-five pounds this week. We have to train your muscles first. Light work. After that, put another ten minutes on the speed bag, alternating hands and that's it for today."

Highland Park, Michigan
The Bag Recreation Center
8:05AM Eastern Standard Time
1959 January 5, Monday

"Good day, not so old man. You're in better shape than I thought," Marcel boasted loudly.

"I'm a Detective, Marcel. We can always run *at least* a mile," Rydon said with a shrug.

"We'll see. Let's go upstairs and talk about the contract."

Walking up the wooden structure of the two-story building, Rydon admired pictures, Championship belts, Iron Fist Awards, newspaper articles, ticket stubs, and tons of other memorabilia. He hadn't been back to the gym since he left for college. The familiar faces lining the walls enlightened him on what he'd missed while he was gone.

Lost in a trance inside a timeless capsule, Marcel brought him back to the present, calling his name from the upstairs office as he hung up the phone.

"You might make it up there with us one day, Champ," Marcel called out.

"Baby steps, Marcel. One day at a time," Rydon said, shadowboxing up the stairs.

"Good attitude! Hard work pays well. This is the contract we're offering you. It's a two-year deal."

"The second year is what we call the *Boxer's Option*. I know you're a married man now, so go over it with the Mrs. and get it back to me by Friday, signed or not."

"I'm a grown man, Marcel. I can make decisions without my wife, sometimes," Rydon responded, looking out the corner of his eye, bluffing as he skimmed the pages.

"Even better!" Marcel clapped, pumping his fists. "Read it over. Let me know if you have any questions. If not, we can get your licensing process started right now."

"You know what? I want Gabby to be with me when I sign it. I'll get it back to you by Friday,"

"Same ole, Donny. You know Gabriella will tell you about yourself if you sign it without her is all I heard." Marcel laughed. "It's going to be good having everyone back in the gym again."

"Yea whatever, potato-potato. Who's everyone?" Rydon asked with peaked curiosity.

"Flash, Ralph Ruh, and Blackout for sure. They're your sparring partners."

"Sparring partners? I haven't boxed live since I was 13. They're heavyweight champions of the world. I need to warm up first. That's like walking with an antelope during a Safari sunset," Rydon said.

"We have time, but we don't have time to waste. Warm up fights would be useless for a person with your skill set," Marcel reminded him.

"I'll spar with the champs after sparing with your best boxers in the gym for a few days. I grew up sparring with Flash, Ruh, and Blackout. I want to see what the young bucks are made of."

"I'll tell you what. Ty Farmer is the real deal but he's just a kid."

"How old is he?"

"Just turned twenty-one in November but he's got power. Fists are big as bricks and his hand-eye coordination is impeccable. He's raw with two left feet and bad defense. But if he lands a haymaker, you might retire a little early," Marcel informed him, watching his fighters train from the office window.

"If he has bad feet, I'd hit him twice before he lands a punch. Not to mention, landing a punch would mean I didn't see his punches coming. My eyes have gotten stronger over the years," Rydon gloated.

"Finally, you understand. Sparring with anyone besides polished boxers is a waste of time. But Farmer could learn a lot from you. Speaking of which, this kid from Louisville stopped by yesterday. Said he's in town for the week and wanted to know if he could train here.

"I don't mind loaning the gym to a traveler for a few days if he's serious about the craft, so I put him to the test. He beat my top three boxers in twenty-seven minutes real time.

"At sixteen years old, he reminded me a lot of you but better. His trash talk was smoother than yours too. It was like poetry. That kid is going to be special. I told him to sign and date the gloves he used. They're hanging up over there. He wrote, *I am the greatest of all time, already!* The kid knows he's badd." Marcel laughed.

"I hope he is better than me. I want to meet him. Make sure he gets all access passes to every fight and that they know to treat him like he's one of us. Did he beat Farmer too?"

"I didn't let him fight Farmer. That could've gotten ugly, either way. I'll let you spar with the gym members over the weekend. After that, I'm throwing you to the wolves."

"I wouldn't have it any other way. I just need to knock off the ring rust. It's been twenty years!"

"It's like riding a bike... that punches."

Rydon squinted his eyebrows, blinking wildly. "Any other concerns give me a call. The contract offer expires Friday, ninety-six hours is standard PBA protocol. They run a tight ship. Unfortunately, you can't box live without a contract so get ready for a lot of cardio and weight training. See you tomorrow at five minutes to six."

"Good deal, brother. Peace."

Highland Park, Michigan
Paradise Condominiums, Manchester Street
10:17AM Eastern Standard Time
1959 January 5, Monday

"Thank you, Ry, you're so thoughtful," she said, taking two large paper cups from Rydon.

Entering a room scented with the aroma of morning breakfast, Gabriella placed two banana kiwi strawberry blends on a table set for two as Rydon took a seat.

"How did you know I would make it in time for breakfast? I know how much you hate cold eggs," Rydon pondered.

"A woman's intuition senses everything," she said with a smile.

"I thought that was a myth."

"Not at all, we know everything."

"Well, Miss Know It All, what's in this envelope?" he asked, holding up his Professional Boxing Association contract.

"A job offering."

"Lucky guess. From whom?"

"A close friend."

"Hmmph," Rydon released, peering out the corner of his eyes. "Two for two. What's my assignment?"

"If I tell you, then I'd have to put my hands on you." She giggled, taking a sip from her straw.

"Hurt me! Hurt me!" Rydon pleaded.

"You are so goofy. What's in the envelope, man. You know I'm nosey."

"Remember when you said I should take a break the other day?

"What else is new?"

"Well, I decided to do it. I'm taking a year and a half off." Rydon smiled, already knowing what she'd say next.

"That's wonderful! We can go to Haiti, Jamaica, the Bahamas, South America, Egypt, Mecca. Baby, we can travel the world in a year and a half. I'm so excited!" Gabriella jumped up from her seat and kissed Rydon on both cheeks.

"Gabby, baby," Rydon said, grabbing her hand. "The early birds win championships."

"What? *The early birds win championships?* What is that supposed mean?" She snickered.

"I'm going to be a professional boxer," he announced quickly and quietly, straightening his mustache with his other hand as he spoke.

"I beg your pardon?" she smirked, with an attitude as she returned to her seat with a slouch.

```
                Highland Park, Michigan
                     John R Street
              5:55AM Eastern Standard Time
                 1959 January 9, Friday
```

After meeting at Manchester and John R Street, Rydon and Marcel jogged south toward Downtown Detroit.

"How you feeling, Champ?"

"I was a little cold a while back. Now I feel like a bronco. Look at my stride. Poster boy material, right?"

"That goes well with your best weapon. Mark my words."

"My stamina?"

"That too, but I was talking about that step back, straight right. Every poster boy needs a signature move. Yours is the *Poster Punch.*"

"The Poster Punch, I like it. I like it a lot, Marcel," Rydon said, throwing hands.

Reaching a dead end, they headed west on Holbrook before continuing south on Woodward Avenue.

"You tired yet, Champ?"

"You're the retired one, you tell me?" Rydon joked, running alongside a childhood friend.

"I'm fine, this is the norm. How far are we going?"

"Let's go to the river and back?"

Finishing the run to the Detroit River, the men reached Jefferson Street, sweating beneath their hats. Piles of snow splashed from the street to the curb with each step they took.

"Now, that was a workout!" Rydon exclaimed.

"How far do you think that was?" Marcel asked.

"Nine or ten miles and we still have to get back home."

"Did you bring your wallet?"

"I have my badge. What's up?"

"Will that get you across the bridge?"

"It can get me in the White House," Rydon replied.

"You always said you'd be top detective. Is it everything you hoped for?"

"It has its days. More money, more problems, have to move carefully. When I'm at work, I still love what I do but it's the people that frustrate me," Rydon explained.

"What makes you say that?"

"Some of the cases I've taken over the years would make you wonder how the world could be so cold and petty."

"I can only imagine. What's the silliest and wildest cases you've ever taken? The ones that made you want to give up on humanity," Marcel inquired.

"That's a good question. Let me think about it for a second," Rydon said, fixing his mustache. "I remember when I was in my twenties, a friend of the family called me to investigate an inside job at a jewelry store her and a college roommate owned together.

"Here's the thing, all three of their employees were up for promotions, but one of them got greedy and tried to get rid of the competition," Rydon said, shaking his head. "That was probably the pettiest."

Rydon pulled his chin hair, as he recollected his thoughts, "A case that made me question these people out here was about a year ago. I was working as an undercover sergeant in a corrupt police force down south in Alabama. The Commissioner for Public Safety calls the shots down there. They treat folks terrible; seen it with my own two eyes."

"Don't you watch television? I could have told you it was bad down there," Marcel said in anguish.

"Not like what I've seen, Marcel. A man sent me an envelope with pictures of people who had been beaten by officers taking orders from the Commissioner. With it, he sent me two checks. One was for fifty thousand dollars. I can't make this stuff up, Marcel.

"The other check was blank and the memo on both checks said *Please help us, Detective Tyme*. It was from a wealthy family who wanted things to go back to the way they were before the Civil Rights War started."

"Did you cash the check?"

"I'll tell you, if you let me talk," Rydon answered, slapping Marcel's bicep with the back of his hand.

"Sorry, man. You always tell stories like the Griots in the African Folklore we used to read at Elmwood. The good ole days. Sometimes I wish I could go back," Marcel said, daydreaming.

"You brought back so many memories. I remember Elmwood. Big Jo was the first person to jam on the rim back in seventh grade."

"He was already six-three," Marcel added.

"Back to the story. I cashed the check. Honestly, just to see if it was legit. Next thing I knew I was leaving with a money bag."

"You still don't have a bank account I see."

"I have a savings account now. Just some money to forget about. The Bank of Highland Park has good interest rates."

"Rydon Tyme has a bank account. I never knew I'd see the day," Marcel said with bulged eyes.

"Me either," Rydon replied. "I'm thinking about getting a couple more. Just for stuff that always comes up on the fly."

"What about the blank check?" Marcel inquired.

"I took the blank check with me to give back to them and ten thousand in cash for emergencies. I met them at the address, knocked on the door and it was an ambush," Rydon said, visibly bothered at the thought of it.

"Are you serious?"

"I can't make this stuff up. It was three of them. I hit the first one with a clean right cross and pulled my pistol on the other two. Cuffed one, zip tied the others and left them there. They said, and I quote, 'When we get out of here, we're going to break you like they used to in the old days, boy!'

"He told me all that with my pistol pointed at him, handcuffed to a seat in whoever's house it was. He had no remorse. Some folks lost all the good in their body. Come to find out, they were jewelers, so the money was legit."

"What did you do with the blank check?"

Removing a folded up piece of paper from underneath the metal clip behind his badge, Rydon handed it to Marcel.

"Is this the blank check!?" he shouted.

"Again, I can't make this stuff up, Marcel," he said, laughing.

"Are you ever going to use it?"

"It's symbolic at this point. Be careful who you trust."

"That's deep."

"But if it ever gets thick... I have at least another fifty grand to fall back on," Rydon joked.

After catching up, Rydon and Marcel finally made their way across the newly constructed Great Lake State Bridge. The bridge offered pedestrian lanes for walkers, runners, bikers, skaters, and automobiles.

It was a part of the United Continents' agenda to make the world a more harmonic place. The United Continents brought leaders of communities across the world together. Twice a year, they discussed how to spend monies earned from global fundraisers.

Continental representation proposed problems identified by citizens of each continent. Every year the United Continents allocated funds to one of the seven continents. The goal was building major attractions to lure tourism and boost the location's economy.

On November 11, 1954, North America chose to build a bridge merging Canada right onto Woodward Avenue of downtown Detroit.

Crossing the bridge over to neighboring Canada, they reached the other side of the Detroit River. Walking along the handrail road, Marcel pointed across the river to the city of Detroit.

"Do you see what I see? "

"The Pentagon Motors building? It does look nice from over here," Rydon replied.

"Close, I see a poster of you on the Pentagon Motors building," Marcel said. "*That's* how to sell a hundred fifty thousand seats. This summer, we're doing a photo shoot right here in this same spot."

"Why wait for the summer when we can do it now?" Rydon asked.

"For one, it's too cold. Two, you're going to need your pistol for a prop. You have to stay true to who you are as a person. You relate to people and you're a highly respected private eye. You can't be an undercover detective for this one. You're starring as THE, Rydon Tyme."

"I've accepted it for what it is, Marcel. You and Jo want me to be a star, I get that. I don't know why, but I get it. What I'm saying is, I have all that now. I keep my badge, camera, and hardware with me at all times."

Changing his sweats for a pair of pants, he removed a pair boxing gloves from his backpack. Rydon covered his boxing trunks that he wore underneath and stood up, holding his dukes for a photo opt.

"You have your piece with you right now?"

"It's in the box in my bag. I'm still a detective even without a case. Just because a teacher retires, doesn't mean they stop teaching, Marcel," Rydon said, throwing jabs to stay warm.

"I hear you loud and clear, brother. But don't call me tomorrow morning saying, you can't make it to the gym because you're too sick. Champs don't get sick."

"No excuses, check. Now hurry up and take the picture. You know how cold it is in Michigan winters without a shirt!?" Rydon exclaimed.

```
Highland Park, Michigan
The Bag Recreation Center
10:34AM Eastern Standard Time
1959 January 9, Friday
```

Returning to a humid gym, felt like a sauna. The two titans conquered mind over matter in a few hours' time. Walking up the decorated stairwell, Marcel and Rydon went back to the round table to talk business.

"What did you think about the contract? Any questions?" Marcel asked, opening negotiations.

"I must have looked over two or three hundred contracts in my life and this is the fairest one I've ever seen. But I do have one question. Why is the purse split so far apart? Seventy to thirty is a huge gap," Rydon asked, taking another look through the proposal.

"Good question. Ultimately, the Professional Boxing Association encourages its boxers to begin self-promoting their own bouts. It puts more money in your pocket now and later on down the line after you retire. It also allows the PBA to invest funds into their rising stars while the household names continue building their brand. Does that make sense?"

"It makes perfect sense." Rydon nodded.

"How did Gabby handle the news?" Marcel wondered, chuckling.

"She thinks it's dumb to let people hit me for money. I tried to tell her that I rarely get hit, but she doesn't like to admit it when she's wrong all the time. Then she said something about not coming home if my face is ever swollen and how I owe her a world tour when this is all said and done."

"That's a great idea, Don. We'll make this a world tour; I'll call Big Jo. Tell Gabriella she's a Genius."

As Rydon exited the gym, Marcel was already on the phone, getting the ball rolling. "Meet me at the spot in fifteen minutes."

"I'll be there," Jo answered.

Highland Park, Michigan
Rocket Park
10:50AM Eastern Standard Time
1959 January 9, Friday

A knock on the passenger side window prompted Marcel to unlock the door. Climbing his six-foot-eight inch frame into Marcel's luxury sedan, Jo immediately pushed his seat back to stretch his cramped legs.

"Big Jo, what's the news?" Marcel asked.

"Just trying to stay free. What's on your mind?" Jo replied in good spirits.

"Have you been charged with anything?"

"No, I just know they've been snooping for a long time."

"Can you leave the country?"

"Always," Jo quickly replied.

"Don and I were thinking about making this thing a world tour. We can promote it ourselves. Four fights will be in the city. We pick opponents to box on the other six continents.

"The United Continents just finished up Palace Stadium in Jerusalem, we could lease it. They're one of the PBA's affiliates. Then we can resurrect the Roman Colosseum."

"He signed the contract?" Jo queried.

"You tell me," Marcel said, handing Jo a manila folder.

Professional Boxing Association: Boxer's Option

The Bag has been approved by the Professional Boxing Association's Board of Trustees and is thereby granted full authority to represent our brand. The Bag is authorized to offer employment to qualified amateur boxers on behalf of the Professional Boxing Association.

Section 1
Healthcare Act:
    a.   The Professional Boxing Association offers lifetime health care benefits to all boxers signed with the company.
Retirement Fund:
    a.   The Professional Boxing Association requires 5% of all earnings from professional bouts, to be paid into the boxer's Retirement Fund.
    b.   Retirement Funds can be disbursed in the following ways:
        1.   One large lump sum.
        2.   Monthly or biweekly increments until funds have been fully disbursed.
        3.   Endorsed to another.
    c.   All boxers are paid annual stipends worth 1% of their total career profits.
    d.   Two tickets are reserved for all retirees wishing to attend Professional Boxing Association events. Reservations begin 24 hours before public sales and are subject to availability afterwards.
    e.   2 tickets to the annual *Boxers Ball*.

Section 2:
Terms of Agreement:
    a.   One season as defined by the Professional Boxing Association is equivalent to ten bouts during a 30 month span.
    b.   *Boxer's Option* guarantees the boxer up to twenty fights. So long as it lasts no longer than 60 months from the date signed on this contract.
    c.   Any and all contract negotiations *must* be completed during the Professional Boxing Association off season (July, August, and September).
    d.   All boxers are required to join the Boxer's Union.

Section 3:
Personal Conduct:
   a. All boxers must entertain the media during press conferences at least once before and after bouts.
   b. Press conferences shall not last longer than 30 minutes unless the boxer consents.
   c. Boxers are expected to act as law-abiding citizens. Misconduct will be handled on a case-by-case basis.

Section 4:
Compensation:
All purses are split 70/30. The event sponsor receives 70%.

I <u>Rydon Tyme</u> accept the terms of this agreement as a boxer of the Professional Boxing Association.

x *Rydon Tyme*   *January 9, 1959*
Professional Boxer

x The Bag Recreation Center 1-9-1959
Witness

"Looks like a signature to me. I knew you'd seal the deal. I'll call him this weekend to let him know what to expect. This world tour idea is phenomenal, absolutely phenomenal," Jo said, clapping his hands.

```
              Highland Park, Michigan
     Paradise Condominiums, Manchester Street
            6:14PM Eastern Standard Time
             1959 January 11, Sunday
```

Inside the four bedroom penthouse, Rydon sat in his office library reading one of his favorite books when the phone rang.

Ring!

"Hello?" Gabriella greeted.

"I got it, baby," Rydon assured her from the phone down the hall.

"Ok, bye bye," she replied.

"Hey, Gabriella, how are you?" Jo asked.

"Hey! J..."

"Don't say my name," Jo said, cutting Gabriella off midsentence.

"Don't say his name," Rydon echoed.

"Hey... you know who you are. I'm doing fine thanks for asking. Goodnight," Gabriella said, laughing as she hung up the phone.

"What's going on, brother?"

"I'm just trying to make the most out of my days," Jo answered.

"Same here, Chief," Rydon agreed.

"I was calling to congratulate you on your new contract and to welcome you to the agency. As your promoter, I will see to it that you sell out every arena no matter the size, every time," Jo promised.

"You two woke a sleeping giant. I've been ready for about a week now."

"That's what I like to hear! Now that you're under contract, gym hours are from 6:00AM to 11:59PM. All PBA boxers are expected to be in shape.

We don't run laps or miles during gym hours. We spar, train, study film, and hit the bag.

"Your first match is in two months. Friday night, March thirteenth, nine o'clock, at The Bag's Auditorium. Live, in front of ten thousand people. We can talk about the specifics later. I'll let you go. If I was a betting man, I'd say you were reading *The Book of One*, Mahdi Amad?"

"Good thing you're not a betting man. I was reading, but it's *Headed West* by Lahal Amunra."

"That was my first guess. Which is exactly why I don't gamble. I second guess myself too much with things I can't control." Jo chuckled.

"March thirteenth. I'll be ready a month early. You can book it," Rydon promised.

"Now that's something I'd bet my last dollar on, every time. Peace, stay safe, brother," Jo said, hanging up the phone.

Highland Park, Michigan
Brother City Broadcasting Company
5:09PM Eastern Standard Time
1959 March 3, Tuesday

Through the main lobby, in the third room on the right. Tempers were flying high in the studio. "For those of you just joining us, we're here with a man set to make his Professional Boxing Association debut. I went to college with this guy when he was a track star. Highland Park's own, Rydon *The Chosen Dreamer* Tyme. Is it the *One* or the *Chosen Dreamer*, Rydon? When I met you, you called yourself HP's Finest. You've got *a lot* of nicknames. Which do you go by most?" the disk jockey asked.

Leaning towards the microphone with a straight face, "Yes," Rydon answered before leaning back in his seat.

"OK..." the host answered slowly, looking awkwardly at his co-host. "We're also here with the former heavyweight champion, a fifteen-year veteran, Delaware *Journeyman* Jefferson. Before we went to commercial, the Chosen Dreamer was just telling us how he was going to win the fight. Do you take back anything you said?"

"If you go to court to fight a speeding ticket and the judge asks you, *Did you speed*, and you reply *Your honor I was running late for work and went twenty over the limit*. He's going to say *guilty*. After that, they move on to the next case. It's too late to take anything back. I said what I said," Rydon declared. "It is what it is."

"As a matter of fact, for those of you who missed what I said," Rydon added, sitting up in his seat to move closer to the microphone. "I'll say it again, right here on the Inner City Traffic Jam Show. This old man doesn't stand a chance against me. I read in the papers he runs five miles a day, I run ten. Fifteen on weekends and twenty just because. I'm quicker than he is, stronger too. He'll be lucky if I let him last five rounds, I'm telling you," Rydon said, warning Journeyman Jefferson as he placed his feet on the desk.

"You sound like a child, rookie. *I'm going to do this and that.* Stop talking about it and do it already, boy!" Delaware said, pounding the table. His fist had already turned red in the last segment from banging on the wood. He was overly frustrated from Rydon's mind games.

44

"You know what. I would like to retract my statement. Forget about the fifth round. You won't make it past the third. I'm going to show you what you just did to yourself the minute you called me boy," Rydon stated as he shrugged, calmly removing his feet from the table.

Diving into his pocket for a piece of paper, Rydon unfolded it loud enough to pop. Immediately, causing the radio personalities to laugh uncontrollably. "Your mouth just wrote a check that your gloves can't cash. You should've stopped while you were at it because one round is all you're lastin'," Rydon shouted, pointing across the table.

"He's promising a first round knockout, in his first fight. Heavyweight boxing is back ladies and gentlemen! The Journeyman looks like he's ready to lace up the gloves right now, people. While the Chosen Dreamer laughs it up with his managers. I wish you could see it," The radio personality said, describing the escalated events to the world.

"That's our time, people. You can buy tickets at The Bag all week until fight night. Act now because they're selling fast. Anything else you two want to say before we go?"

"You started your career against the wrong old guy. You're going down for the count, boy," Delaware said, grunting.

"I said what I said. Get there early folks, or else you might miss this one. This clown is going down in the first round, less than three minutes after the bell sounds.

"I'm going to hit him with a left then a right. Pop him with a Poster Punch to end the fight. As he crashes to the canvas, I need you all to ignite--- with chants of *goodnight*," Rydon requested, removing his Lethal Lenses from his pocket as he sported the sunglasses indoors.

"He's poetic too. Ladies, he's so dreamy. The name fits him well," the co-host reported, star struck by Rydon's presence.

"Easy, Phillis. He's a happily married man," Theodore said, holding his microphone.

"Yea, easy, Phillis. You're going to get me in trouble. I'm glad there aren't any cameras here to catch me blushing. Gabby, I'm sorry but she's beautiful. What was I thinking? I'm really in trouble now," Rydon said, slapping his forehead.

"Sorry..." Phillis dragged out.

"It's alright, Phillis. Gabby knows Beany isn't going anywhere. But now that you mention it; hey, chump, you want to know why they call me the Chosen Dreamer? It's because I'm choosing to haunt you in your sleep. Once that bell rings, shortly after, shhhhh... not a peep!" Rydon shouted with laughter.

Delaware Jefferson had to be restrained after being psychologically manipulated. Through it all, Rydon was having a ball at Journeyman Jefferson's expense, taking the upper hand early on.

Detroit, Michigan
Davison and Broadstreet Avenue
3:13PM Eastern Standard Time
1959 March 13, Friday

A once vacant parking lot, hosted hundreds of the Brother City's finest talents, ready to shake up the two cities with an unexpected surprise.

March thirteenth would forever be recognized as Brother City Day. The day both Detroit and Highland Park put on a joint event, parading it down the Davison Freeway. On a date they would soon share an area code with.

Ticket sales weren't close to capacity. In efforts to pack the house, Marcel, Jo, and Rydon launched the inaugural, Davison Freeway Parade. Dozens of marching bands from across the state warmed up for their performance to the ticket boxes.

"You ready, Champ?" Jo asked, ready to get things started.

"I was born ready. The doctor was so surprised, I had to slap *him*," Rydon replied.

"I have officially heard it all."

Jo and Marcel rallied the troops, guiding participants to their designated formations.

"Victory High School Marching Band, winners of last year's Battle of the Bands, you're first in line followed by Highland Park City High. Michigan International University, Atlantis Campus is third before the Generals of Revere High, then Justice High.

Peninsula State University you're next, Go U'pers! We haven't forgotten about you. Dancers, I need you all here behind Elmwood Elementary..."

With the pieces in place, it was time to put the pedal to the metal. The Drumline led the way, commanding the attention of everyone in the area. Rydon arranged for squad cars to escort anyone joining them on their journey across town.

Elders of the community smiled, marveling at the native son stepping into a new venture, while watching from the front lawns of their homes.

Paperboys returning from their routes rode ahead, spreading the news of his arrival. It was a Friday night affair and the whole city was invited.

"What's going on up here?" a man asked from his car, stuck at a stop sign.

"He wants to know what's happening," Rydon announced to the crowd.

"A man is going down in the first round!" they all answered.

People were lured by the words coming from Rydon's megaphone. By the time the parade crossed Dexter Avenue, hundreds were already lined up to join. Over a half hour into the show, numerous call and response chants had been created to the cadences of the state's top marching bands.

"He wrote a check that his gloves can't cash and called me a boy. His only way out the ring is hitting the floor. We can stop here--- or do you want more?" Rydon spoke through the mouthpiece, jogging through the neighborhood.

"More! More! More!" the crowd roared.

Reaching Linwood Street, their following multiplied in bunches.

"They call him the Journeyman. After he loses, we're going to send him on the road again. My punches are soothing, leave him drooling--- goodnight!"

"Goooooooooooooood Niiiiiiiiiiiiiiiiight,

Goooooooooooooood Niiiiiiiiiiiiiiiiiight," they all chanted.

Passing Rosa Parks Boulevard, they continued to Woodward Avenue, where they went north. The party arrived at one of the box office locations on Manchester Street. With thousands in attendance, lines formed at the box offices where hats and t-shirts were passed out with ticket purchases.

Smiling in approval of their accomplishment, Rydon had one more thing to say. "Thank you for coming. I really appreciate your support. I just wish you all were going to witness a longer fight. I'm going to end it quick, people," he said as the crowd laughed.

"I'll make you proud tonight. Not only will I give you a good show, but the after-party is on me. Bring your dancing shoes. I repeat, stick around after the fight. The after-party is on me.

"Shuttles are headed back and forth to Broadstreet for the rest of the day in case anybody has to get some shopping done. We brought you all this way, we're not going to leave you stranded," Rydon said jokingly as the crowd laughed.

"If you want to head to The Bag now, you can. The Battle of the Bands starts at five o'clock. Next door to The Bag at the high school on the fifty-yard line. They've got the grills fired up already and your ticket gets you a plate." The crowd laughed again as one woman chimed in. "You know I'm hungry."

"Me too," Rydon said, chuckling. "That was a long walk, but you did that. *We* did that, y'all. Give yourself a hand." Rydon peered out into the crowd, seeing many faces of hope. His reputation as a detective gave him a puncher's chance in the eye of the public not knowing his background in the sport.

"We've got Big Bus Transportation across the street if you've been standing too long, and your feet hurt. They'll be trailing behind the band in ten minutes.

"Take it easy, everyone. I have to finish warming up. Thanks again!"

"Alright nah," one replied as they chattered amongst themselves.

Thousands of Brother City residents cheered on as Rydon jogged off with Marcel down the street to the gym. Relying on The Bag's reputation, boxing fans across the city knew a champion when they saw one.

```
        Highland Park, Michigan
          The Bag, Auditorium
      8:55p Eastern Standard Time
         1959 March 13, Friday
```

Sitting on a massage table with one hand wrapped and gloved, Rydon's other hand trembled uncontrollably. The sports tape being wrapped around his hands folded in half, preventing it from sticking.

"Nervous?" Marcel asked sarcastically.

"Is it that obvious?" Rydon asked.

"Sweaty hands, you can't keep steady enough for me to do my job. Nope, I would have never guessed it."

"I don't know what's wrong, Marcel. I've never been nervous before a match."

"Don't tell me you're scared of the Journeyman?" Marcel asked, intentionally pressing Rydon's buttons.

"I fear no one but One, and it's not that bum. I haven't fought competitively in twenty years, Marcel. My arms feel heavy. I can't keep my hands still and I have RLS," Rydon diagnosed.

"RLS?" Marcel asked with confusion.

"Restless leg syndrome." Rydon shrugged.

"It's probably because you talked so much. I've never heard you talk trash talk *outside* the ring before," Marcel said, laughing.

"I'm a grown man now, brother. A lot has changed. I wasn't going to go as far as I did until he called me *boy* on the radio. After that, I had to set an example for the other nine boxers on the schedule."

"I shook my head as soon as he said it. Well, it's time to hit the ring, ready or not," Marcel warned, punching Rydon's gloves.

"You know me better than that. I was born ready with a badge and mustache."

Making his way to the locker room, Jo ducked his head underneath the doorway, avoiding a minor concussion. "Come here, Big Jo," Marcel called out.

After Marcel placed Rydon's hands into Jo's, it caused a sudden upper body jerk. "Don't tell me the Journeyman has you shook, Champ," Jo asked, calmly pushing him.

"Not in a million years. I don't know why I'm so nervous," Rydon said, shaking his head.

"Me either, but you're kicking your feet like a third grader, *boy*," Jo said, pushing him further.

At an instant, Rydon's hands steadied as his feet came to a halt. "Uh-oh, he's seeing red now. You made the man angry, Big Jo." Marcel smiled, already thinking ahead of what he'd wear for the after-party.

"Good, let's go! We have places to be and people to beat," Jo said on his way back to the boxing ring, adjusting the lapels on his suit.

Walking down the hallway leading to The Bag's auditorium, Rydon glanced at the pictures hanging on the walls while warming up the Poster Punch. Cheers from the crowd could be heard yards away from the entrance, as his introduction music played to the cadence of his footsteps.

His Poster Punch turned to rapid fists of fire and furious flurries. Soon, he was bouncing from side to side, swinging hooks and uppercuts. Shadow boxing at full speed, Marcel and Jo looked at each other smiling from ear to ear.

"And now, the moment you've all been waiting for. It's time for the main event. Making his way to the ring wearing white trunks and black gloves, weighing in at two hundred and seven pounds. Standing six feet tall from the City of Trees, the hometown hero, Rydon the Chosennnnn Dreammmmmmmer Tyme!"

Playing to the crowd, Rydon cupped his gloved hand to his ear as he entered the boxing ring.

Locking eyes with his favorite woman sitting ringside, he winked with a wave, catching the air kiss she sent his way.

"Up next, weighing in at two hundred and twenty-six pounds, standing six-foot-five inches with an eighty inch wingspan; by way of Vidor, Texas. Dressed in the orange trunks and red gloves, former heavyweight champion of the world--- I introduce to you, Delaware Journeyman Jefferson!"

Both men entered the ring drenched with sweat. Walking to the center of the square, their faces were full of wrinkles. Viciously staring each other down, Rydon cracked a smile at the Journeymen immediately after receiving rules and expectations from the referee.

"Touch gloves. Let's make history, the right way fellas," the referee instructed.

Heading to the corner, Rydon knew his next trip out would be the real deal. Raising his right glove to the sky, he tapped his heart with his left glove, bouncing from side to side.

Round One

Tyme sizes up his opponent, circling around him. It looks like he's on a merry-go-round out there. We're thirty seconds into the fight and neither of the two has thrown a punch. If you all missed the Inner-City Traffic Jam Show last week, you may be thinking, Rydon Tyme can talk the talk but right now, he can't walk the walk.

A minute deep into a fight promised to end in just two more minutes, there still hasn't been any punches thrown. It feels like I'm watching a live game of Chess and the fans feel the same. They are starting to let them hear about it.

"Boooooooooo!"

"Stop stalling!"

"Throw a punch!"

Whoa! Here we go, action! Tyme capitalized on a missed right hook from the Journeyman, responding with a left of his own to the body. He faints with a left jab, landing another big blow to the body! The Chosen Dreamer just woke up and so did the crowd!

I stand corrected. Tyme can definitely walk the walk, folks. Another swing and a miss by the Journeyman. If it had landed, this one may have been over. Up against the ropes is Tyme. The Journeyman has him right where he wants him. I'm telling you, folks, he's landing damaging combinations, but Tyme doesn't look at all phased.

"Is that all you've got, little buddy?" Rydon spoke to him mid fight.

There's the mouth we've been hearing about. Tyme continues to taunt the Journeyman who has him pinned against the ropes halfway through the first round.

"Hit me!" Rydon yelled.

This guy Tyme is fearless. Those punches must hurt coming from those big boulders of the Journeyman.

"This is your last chance. Stop tickling me and fight, chump!" Rydon berated.

I know he has a few nicknames already, but I'll add another to the list. The Mighty Mouth because you cannot shut this man up.

"Goodnight, little buddy," Rydon told him as they grappled.

Tyme bounces off the ropes with a minute left in the first. Looks like he's back on offense. What a right hand to the face by the Mighty Mouth. He steps back but not before landing a nice 1-2 combination with a well-placed left uppercut to the chin. The Journeyman looks a little dazed after that jazzy combination, folks. Do you folks at home watching on television see this man's hand speed?

Twenty seconds left in the round. Tyme inches closer. Great reflexes dodging another jab from the Journeyman. Wait a second. Tyme bounces back like a bunny rabbit and lands a straight right hand.

Wobble, wobble, wobble look at those knees! Tyme sees it too because here comes another flurry.

Left jab, left hook, body, body. Another straight right to the head. The man has plenty of power in both hands.

Tyme leans out of the way of a wild punch by the Journeyman. Uh-oh! This might be it. He's bouncing backwards again. What a right hand by Tyme! Oh my! Oh my! The Journeyman is down! I repeat the Journeyman has hit the road!

If this is it, we may be witnessing greatness manifesting right before our eyes.

"1... 2... 3... 4... 5... 6... 7... 8... 9... 10. You're out!"

Ding! Ding! Ding! Ding! Ding! Ding! Ding!

Ladies and gentlemen, the Chosen Dreamer may be the One after all. I think that's the nickname I'll stick with after a fight like that. I cannot believe what I just witnessed. These fans are ecstatic. Oh my, listen to the people, listen to the people!"

Goooooooooooooood Niiiiiiiiiiiiiiiiight!

Goooooooooooooood Niiiiiiiiiiiiiiiiight!

The Journeyman doesn't know where he is right now. He looks lost and confused. I think it's safe to say that was the Poster Punch we've heard so much about. Wow, what a fight! I'm sure that picture will be enlarged for a wall near you.

On behalf of channel seventy-seven and Brother City Broadcasting, I'm Scott Wilcox. Thank you for joining us, goodnight. No pun intended.

Highland Park, Michigan
The Bag, Northwest Corridor
10:52p Eastern Standard Time
1959 March 13, Saturday

After countless interviews, photo opts and the post-bout press conference, Rydon noticed a figure standing in the shadows along his jog to the locker room. "This would have ended a lot differently if we were in Vidor," a voice called from the darkness.

Slowing to a halt, Rydon stopped and turned around. "What! Did you just threaten me?" he shouted.

"This late at night, if we were back home. I would have to call it a promise, boy. Your kind don't win fights gainst' the Journeyman in Texas," the man said with two younger, stronger men behind him.

Plunk!

Rydon thumped the man in the middle of the forehead. The force of the strike caused a knot that bruised and reddened almost instantly. "Don't you ever in your life, threaten me. You understand!?" Rydon yelled, pushing the man's forehead with his first finger.

"Ahhh!" the man wailed. "Don't just stand there, get him," he yelled at his goons.

"Get me, I dare you!" Rydon roared, flinching at the man who started it all, causing him to tremble in fear of an attack. "Look at him. That's your leader, you take orders from this half of a man? Y'all go through what we go through out there and this is who you work for?" Rydon said, disgusted at the two youngsters.

"Come with me, I'll make you great," Rydon proposed with a fist bump.

The goons seemed hesitant. Unsure of who to follow at the moment, considering the circumstances. The shift of power they witnessed made them see things for what they really were. A very effective reality check.

"You, get up!" Rydon pointed to the leader of the group who was still rubbing his skin. "Go show whoever you work for your forehead and tell them, they're next... Get out of here!" he said, shooing him.

The man tripped over himself, falling to the ground as he scurried away. Holding his frontal lobe, Rydon's thump left a burgundy, half dollar sized hematoma. "You two, follow me. Let's go, keep up. Walk and talk," Rydon commanded as he left for the locker room.

"You, what's your name?" Rydon asked, pointing to the stockier man.

"Flip."

"Big Flip, why did you take orders from that coward?" Rydon asked.

"He has a lot of money and connections in high places where we're from."

"That doesn't answer my question. Why was he your boss is what I'm asking?"

"I wanted the same things, you could say."

"Does he give you any money?"

"Sometimes."

"Does he take you to meetings and show you how the game works?"

"No."

"So why are you listening to a man who isn't teaching you how to grow without him? He was using you and you let him do it. How are you going to make the kind of money he makes if he's not showing you the ropes?

"One of the most important things I've learned in this crazy world is, a man can make money, but money can never make a man. It can mask insecurities, but it can't make you a man."

"Deep. That's heavy," Flip agreed.

"Have you ever seen him act like that before?"

"No, sir."

"See what I mean. Stick around and you might learn something. I'll teach you how to get your own riches."

Squeezing his eyebrows together, Rydon had a sudden epiphany. "That's a four-thirty-three. Wait here. I'll be back," Rydon said, taking off in a sprint.

Chasing after the man he sent away minutes ago, Rydon caught up to him and grabbed him by the collar near the end of the hallway. "You are under arrest for jeopardizing the safety of a law enforcement agent without presence of malicious unjust treatment."

"But you're a boxer, not a cop."

"True, facts only. But I am a detective, and you work for me now."

"I thought that was just a gimmick!" the man shouted, fearfully.

```
            Highland Park, Michigan
              The Bag, East Ballroom
        11:39PM Eastern Standard Time
            1959 March 13, Saturday
```

Opening the door to the east ballroom of The Bag Recreational Center, Rydon was greeted by a huge ovation from a host of family, friends, and supporters.

Goooooooooooooooood Niiiiiiiiiiiiiiight!

Goooooooooooooooood Niiiiiiiiiiiiiiight!

"A man went down in the first round!" Rydon shouted, pumping his fist.

The room was full of love and respect for one of the city's most promising residents. Like clockwork, the one who stood out was his angel in disguise. Wearing another knockout gown made of the finest Italian silk. His prize for life hugged him with a kiss, holding his face with both hands.

"You kissed me like you missed me," Rydon flirted.

"I did, and this is for winning tonight," she said planting another kiss.

"Get a room you two," Jo interrupted.

"Goodbye," Gabriella said, flipping her hair. "I guess I can let you have him for a little while," she waved, walking away.

"I'll bring him back in one piece. I promise," Jo replied with his right hand up.

"I'm going to hold you to that," she said pointedly.

"It's about time you showed up. Did you see the guy Secret Seven just took out of here? He had a third eye, man. Right in the middle of his forehead. It winked at a few folks. He must have owed somebody a lot of money," Jo joked.

"That's why I'm late," Rydon admitted.

"You knotted because he owed you money?" Jo asked with his eyes bulged.

"I did what I did because he threatened my life, and my hands were still wrapped and taped. I just thumped him, that's all. He was arrested for committing a four thirty-three. My guess is he's in Jefferson's entourage."

"And they say you're the nice one. I keep telling people *I'm* really the nice one," Jo insisted, with his thumbs pointed at himself. "I'm glad you and your thumping hand are ok."

"I'm always alright, brother, even when I'm not," Rydon reminded him.

"Even when I'm not. I know," Jo echoed. "Great fight tonight, Champ. You looked better than Masterful himself out there if you ask me. But no one asked me. So, stew on that."

"Thanks, Big Jo. That means a lot coming from you."

"I just call it like I see it. You know the people think you're in your early twenties? One guy told me *Imagine how good he'll be in his thirties.* You woke up the city. The sky is the limit from here.

"I know we're off the clock so I'll be brief. Tonight's official number in attendance was ten thousand, one hundred and forty-three."

"Nice," Rydon admired.

"The phones have been ringing off the hook. Everyone wants you on their schedule. How often are you looking to box?"

"I just want a month to myself after every match, that's all I ask. I can be ready for any fight in two months or less."

"Three months apart, maybe less. It's done. We don't have an opponent yet, but we set a date and found a venue."

"You must be jiving."

"When have you ever known me to jive about making money? I'm a businessman," Jo said.

"I apologize. I almost forgot who I was talking to!" Rydon shouted excitedly, still hyped from his professional debut.

"Don't beat yourself up about it. Just don't let it happen again. Save the date, Saturday, May ninth over at the Civil Center on Eight Mile and Van Dyke."

"That place holds twenty something thousand people, Jo."

"Twenty-five thousand, three hundred is what the Fire Marshal cleared but who's counting seats."

"You don't think it's too early trying to boost attendance one hundred fifty percent?"

"The early birds win championships. I keep telling you that."

New Delhi, India
World International Airport
6:14AM India Time Zone
1959 April 5, Sunday

"I love this sari. This gold and turquoise are out of sight."

"It is. We need to get you on a runway modeling silk. You make it look so good," Rydon said, brushing his hands across the fabric.

"Aww, thank you."

A month in India gave the Tyme's a chance to enjoy each other and the many attractions they visited. Ancient tombs, the Taj Mahal, and many others were all captured in real time with the shutter of a camera lens.

The day he shared the news of his intentions to box professionally, he agreed to terms with Gabriella as well. One month after each fight was to be spent navigating the world during his time off.

"I'm not ready to go back."

"I told you this would be a good idea," she countered.

Highland Park, Michigan
The Bag Recreational Center
9:45AM Eastern Standard Time
1959 April 13, Monday

"Look what the wind blew in," Marcel said, greeting Rydon as he entered the upstairs office.

"What's up, Thumps?" Jo laughed, holding his stomach.

"Jo is the real Mighty Mouth. He told half the gym. Three people asked me about that from the door to the second floor. Did you all hear that one yet, Mighty Mouth?" Rydon responded, shaking his head as he walked by, giving his newspaper away.

"Scott Wilcox gave it to you. It's catchy and it fits. Did you hear about the guy Secret Seven arrested?"

"Which one?" Rydon asked.

"The one with three eyes," Jo said, laughing louder and louder.

"Here you go," Rydon answered. "I walked right into it," he said, shaking his head once again. "What about him?"

"He's loaded, a multimillionaire. One of the kingpins in the jewelry industry," Jo said, bringing him up to speed.

"I never got to question him. I forgot he existed, honestly," Rydon finished as he shrugged. "The jewelry business seems to be a common denominator lately.

"They put a lot of money behind some of these fighters as silent investors."

"I'm glad you told me. I need to give him call. You need anything?" Rydon asked. "Jo, Marcel?"

"Is that a trick question? I'll take a gold Linx watch and a couple of gold rope chains," Jo replied.

"I'm definitely seeing a gold Linx watch in my future," Marcel said, grabbing his left wrist where he would place the timepiece.

"I think we have ourselves a silent sponsor," Rydon chuckled.

"Apparently he's in the Journeyman's entourage," Marcel added.

"He *was* in the Journeyman's entourage. He works for me now. How did you get his profile?" Rydon asked.

"It was on the Midnight News. He claimed he got the bruise during a store robbery but of course the cameras weren't recording at the time. He didn't mention your name either."

"Of course not, he was in the wrong. I just finished what he started," Rydon replied.

"It gets ugly behind the scenes, Don. This is just the beginning," Marcel warned him. "Tom Claxton called Big Jo today. The Journeyman wants a rematch in Vidor," Marcel said, giving Rydon an update on his current schedule.

"Texas? Are you serious?" Rydon asked,

"I'm always serious," Marcel answered.

"I'm just surprised he'd ask for a home rematch after going down in the first round," Rydon replied, admiring his fists.

"He said you got lucky because the crowd was so one-sided," Marcel added.

"We'd have to have the city with us in a place like that," Jo reminded them.

"Secret Seven is everywhere, brother. Every state, every continent. We'll be fine. Rydon answered without worry.

"I forget I'm not just talking to the Mighty Mouth but THE Rydon Tyme!" Jo said, with his hands up as they left the office, headed downstairs to the gym.

"I'm the same Rydon from Manchester and Oakland. Don't let the media fool you, brother," he humbly retorted.

"I hear you, Champ. Warm up on the bag for thirty minutes then get ready for Flash. He's coming in at noon. Jo, come back to the office with me for a second," Marcel said, already halfway up the stairs.

For the first time in over half a decade, Rydon felt alive again, having control of his own fate. Boxing was his favorite past time while growing up in the 1930s. Being back in the gym after years of absence, restored his love and passion for the sport.

Flash Shabazz was Rydon's mentor and sparring partner until Rydon left high school early for college. The two were on pace to becoming The Bag's best products.

Beginning his professional career as an eighteen-year-old welterweight, Flash Shabazz went on to win his first championship belt at twenty years and one month.

At twenty-five, he moved twenty-seven wins and zero losses to the middleweight division. Four months before his thirty-first birthday, Shabazz added win number forty on the night he acquired the Middleweight Championship Belt.

Toward the end of his career, Flash bulked up to enter the heavyweight division. He retired in 1958. One day after making Professional Boxing Association history as the first boxer to hold a championship belt in four different weight classes. While breaking the record for most wins without a loss at fifty-seven.

"Flash!" someone shouted.

Bursting through the doors, commanding the room's attention, stood five-foot-ten, two hundred pounds, Flash Shabazz. Accompanied by his favorite reporters and busloads of honor roll students from school districts across the state, Flash successfully paused the workday.

"So, it is true. You're finally joining the greats?" Flash smiled, removing his sunglasses.

"Flash, how's life, brother?" Rydon asked with a handshake and man hug.

"I can't complain. I haven't seen you in the gym since we were their age," Flash answered.

"Time flies and what are you all doing here? You're supposed to be in school," Rydon said, squinting his eyebrows.

"See y'all, I told you we were friends. Everybody say, *It's Spring Break, Donny, loosen up.*"

"It's Spring Break, Donny, loosen up!" they all replied.

"That's Mr. Donny to you!" Rydon said, pointing with his gloved mitts.

One of Rydon's biggest support groups were those who weren't yet old enough to vote. Ever since taking his first case, he visited schools in whatever district he worked in.

Every morning, he volunteered his services until he had seen every school in the district. Over the years he watched them all grow up in front of his eyes like a niece or nephew.

"I'm here for your pre-bout press conference. They didn't they tell you?" Flash smiled.

"I had no clue. I thought you were coming to spar." Rydon chuckled.

"You thought I came to spar? Slow down, Donny. I'm retired. Besides, you're still a little wet behind the ears. I'll spar with you further down the line. Today, I'm here to ask you a few questions with the little ones, are you ready?"

"Can a polar bear swim? Of course, I'm ready," Rydon answered jabbing the bag.

"This question is from Gary, a third grader from Kalamazoo City Elementary," Flash announced, reading a flash card.

"Who taught you how to box?" Little Gary asked. Juice stains decorated Gary's shirt. He was mid sip when he heard his name being called to talk to the person who inspired him to box just weeks earlier.

"Good question," Flash added.

"That is a good question. That's a difficult question. A lot of people have taught me a lot of things. My grandfather introduced me to the sport. Fun fact, his grandfather, which would be my great, great grandfather was one the founders of this recreation center. Another fun fact so was Flash's great, great grandfather.

"Wowwwwwww!" they all said in unison,

"I know, pretty cool, right?"

"My grandpa teaches me about boxing too!" Gary shouted.

"Wowwwwwww!" Rydon replied. "How old are you, Gary?"

"Nine."

"Stick with it, Gary. I need you to be better than me. You got it, Gary?"

Gary shook his head up and down. Stuck in awe, he was no longer able to speak.

"But back to your question Gary, from K-Zoo. My father was my first trainer. He taught me most of what I know. These two champions to my left and right taught me more than they'll ever know. A young man from Louisville no older than some of you all taught me how to have fun again."

"Glad I could help," Flash replied on his way to the next question. "From what I hear, you'll be a Champion one day soon. Our next question is from Lance, a fifth grader from Garvey Elementary up north on I-75 in Saginaw."

"Is it harder being a boxer or a detective?" A chunk of Rydon's newest supporters only knew him to be a boxer. His days as a Detective were becoming urban legends.

"Wow, you all are asking some great questions. I hope you reporters in the back are taking notes. They're setting the bar pretty high!

"That's one of the best questions I've ever been asked. People seem to forget that I'm a detective. I have a different answer today than I would've had a year ago. Boxing is easier for me but that's because I'm a workaholic. In boxing, you somewhat control your own destiny. When did that man go down?"

"In the first round!" they all replied.

"That was weak. I'm louder than all of you and it's just me. When!?"

"In the first round!!!" they all shouted.

"The three minutes that it took to whoop that man required three months of training. Marcel and I ran ten to fifteen miles a day, through the snow sometimes, in boots! I sparred with giants like big ole Ty Farmer over there.

"Plus, hours of jumping rope, lifting weights, and punching the bag like I was when you all walked in. I did all of that to look good for a three minute fight. It only looks easy because I'm very passionate about what I do," Rydon answered.

"Our last question is from Paul, a kindergartner from Seven Mile Elementary in the Brother City of Detroit."

"Do you want to spar with me?" the little boy challenged.

"Paul, is that you? Why you always calling me out? Yea, I'll spar with you. I bet I can take you too!" Rydon charged.

"Nuh unnn!"

"That's it I've had enough of you. Put up your dukes!"

The audience laughed on a dime as Rydon went toe to toe with his mini foe. Experiencing the first knockdown of his early career, he tumbled to the canvas. The crowd of grade school students aged four to eighteen, roared when he sprung to his feet, lifting young Paul to sit atop his broad shoulders.

"Hey, Paul, you hit harder than the Journeyman," Rydon joked. "Boys and girls, Flash and Paul are going to lead you all to the auditorium. I'll be down after I shower. Does that sound like a plan?"

"Yayyyyy!!!" they all rejoiced.

Highland Park, Michigan
The Bag, Auditorium
12:38PM Eastern Standard Time
1959 April 13, Monday

Making his way to the podium, Rydon shook hands all the way to the microphone.

"What's the news?"

"The news is good," the crowd responded.

"Good, peace be with you. That's what I like to hear. I was so surprised to see you all today, I wasn't expecting this at all. Looks like we have more people here too, which means you all have been helping each other out. Give yourselves a hand." Rydon paused during the applause.

"How many people do we have here today, Flash?" Rydon asked, turning to his long-time friend.

"They are two-thousand and five strong!"

"That's a lot of people. Last semester it was a little less than a thousand. That's a one hundred percent increase, plus."

Frozen in his speech Rydon looked over to Jo and pointed up sending him a message.

"I'm proud of you all. Let your parents know their tickets are on me. They'll be two out of fifty thousand people to watch me beat up the next guy. Tell the world! Let everyone know, even the guy I'm fighting. You want to know why?"

"Why!?" they responded.

"Because I'm the best in the Midwest, to the press, I have no competition and I mean everything I say. Shhhh--- listen. Four rounds of my time, that's all I'm giving him."

"But Tyme you don't know who you're fighting yet. What happens if you win in five rounds, or if he beats you?

"There are no what ifs. You'll be walking out the door after I drop him in four," Rydon promised.

"Insiders are saying you may end up facing Emory, Connor, or Melzi, your thoughts?"

"It doesn't matter who it is. Especially those mediocre boxers you just mentioned and please no bulletin board material questions. They're getting dry and outdated. You're much more creative than that. It's 1959, people. Step it up."

"Word is, you talk so brashly to mask your fears. Any truth behind that?" one reporter asked.

"I fear no one but One. I talk this way because I am the only person who can beat me. My story is already written, next question?"

"Will you be ready for another fight so soon?" another queried.

"I was born ready. I've been ready for so long, I got bored and went to the future--- watched the fight, came back and told you I'd drop him in the fourth round," Rydon predicted, as the assembly of reporters broke out in laughter. "Next, yes?" he pointed.

"What's your favorite car and what color?" a young man questioned.

"That was a curve ball. What's your name and what made you ask me that?"

"Titus Attucks, intern reporter from the Highland Park Sun. The questions I have written down have already been asked and it was the first thing to come to mind, Tyme."

"Clever. You're hired. I want you to be my personal writer. You think differently, and I appreciate that. To all you people out there in TV land. If you miss any of my interviews, you can read them in Titus Attucks' column.

"To answer your question, I'm a Pentagon man. They look nice, ride smooth as a boat and tough as a tank. My favorite has to be either a blue Passion, an Eternal in silver, or any of their trucks."

Detroit, Michigan
The Buffalo Dome, Mack Avenue
9:00PM Eastern Standard Time
1959 May 9, Saturday

Alright people this is the moment we've all been waiting for. The night we get to see if Rydon Tyme is as good as advertised. He sure can draw a crowd, that's for sure. The eight-thirty count, was forty-five thousand. People are marching in like ants on a sugar mission. The only question is, who are they cheering for? The Mighty Mouth or current Number One Contender, Mavis Melzi?

Here we go folks, it's time for the main event.

"Ladies and gentlemen, this heavyweight contest is scheduled for fifteen rounds. Weighing in at six feet even, two hundred pounds, in the black trunks, red gloves. From the Brother City of Highland Park, Rydon *The Mighty Mouth* Tyme!" the announcer called to the crowd.

Listen to that crowd. I haven't seen a following this strong in ages.

"In the red, white, and blue striped trunks, from Decatur, Mississippi. Standing six feet, one inch, two hundred ten pounds. Your Number One Contender, Mavis *Manic!* Melzi!" the announcer shouted.

"You know the rules. We talked about them in the locker room. Keep those punches where I can see them. Let's make history the right way men, touch gloves," the referee instructed.

Would you look at that, Mavis doesn't want to touch gloves with the Mighty Mouth. I've never seen this before, and I don't know if Tyme is the guy you want mad at you before a fight.

"Melzi, we're waiting on you!" the referee said, losing patience.

Manic finally touches gloves with Tyme. I can't believe what I'm seeing. Manic is wiping his gloves on his trunks as if they've become tainted by Tyme's mitts.

Oh brother, look at the Mighty Mouth. He is disgusted. He's not smirking today. He's pointing and shouting at Manic so loud they can scribe his words from the press boxes. This should be a good one. It's scheduled for

71

fifteen, Tyme predicted four but as angry as he is right now, we may witness another first round knockout.

Round One

There you have it folks, it's ShowTime on the east side of Detroit. Blowing steam like a locomotive, Tyme seems to be taking a different approach for this fight. The first punch is a missed left jab from Tyme countered with a right hook to the head by Mavis the Manic.

Tyme steps back but Manic is on him like an orange peel, pinning him in the corner with another hook to the face, followed by a left and a right to the body. Tyme swings wildly but misses again as Mavis the Manic lights him up with a strong jab. The Mighty Mouth may have met his match folks, it's not looking good for him.

Finally making his way out of the corner, Tyme looks a little queasy out there, folks. Looks like a game of cat and mouse, honestly. Tyme's backing up like he's parallel parking, wow! There's that poster punch we've grown to love. Tyme follows with a flurry of blows to the midsection. Manic pushes him off and seems unaffected by that strong combination.

Ding! Ding!

That's the end of round one folks and I must say, Tyme looks lost out there. Nothing like the fighter we saw a couple months ago. I wish I could vouch for him ladies and gents, but I've only seen him box two total rounds and today, he's only landed seven of the twenty-two punches he's thrown. Not only that, but he's getting lit up by Manic. I wouldn't lie to you folks.

Round Two

I'm anxious to see what Tyme has left in his tank. A name like Mighty Mouth can be bittersweet, we're starting to see. Tyme is circling the ring, moving this way and that. Funny how fast things change. What once looked like planned precision now seems like he's running from his opponent.

"Boo!!!"

"Wake up, Tyme!"

"Watch that right hand!"

Bam!

Tyme's corner tried warning him about that strong right cross headed his way. What an upper cut by Manic that knocks Tyme against the ropes. That one stunned him. The ropes may have saved him from the first knockdown of his career.

The two boxers are now circling each other in the middle of the ring. Tyme throws another telegraphed right hook as Manic answers with a right hand uppercut.

We're halfway through the second round and Mad Man Manic has silenced the Mighty Mouth, absorbing his punches like photosynthesis. I don't know how many more of these uppercuts Tyme can take and those knees? Don't get me started. They're like jelly, folks.

Call it luck if he makes it out the second round the way he's fighting. Tyme's corner is screaming directions to him at this point while he circles the ring. He's doing his own thing tonight and it's not working well for him.

Nice left jab by Tyme. Another left and right, left hook.

"You're terrible," Rydon insulted.

Uh-oh, here comes the Mighty Mouth.

"Your best shot isn't good enough, little buddy," Rydon said, taunting.

"Shut up," Mavis snapped back.

A right, left, right flurry by Tyme. I think the lion is awake!

Manic runs right into a planted left jab and another left before Tyme retreats, uh-oh, here it comes... What a Poster Punch by Tyme! That may have been the best punch of this young boxer's early career.

One thing I will say about Tyme is that his composure reminds me of the late great David Sampson from back in the early twenties. Nothing seems to rattle him no matter how many punches he's been hit with. He's got a fighter's spirit that's for certain.

With ten seconds left in the second, Manic is still charging like the bell just rang. What a combination to the body by Manic.

Ding! Ding!

Manic must have sand in his ears because he's not letting up.

Ding! Ding! Ding! Ding! Ding!

He's still going!

Ding! Ding! Ding! Ding! Ding! Ding!

It's a good thing we have referees like Big Ole Wellington Owens.

"Melzi, I don't care how mad you are. You pull another stunt like that, and I'll jab you myself. This is my ring, and you play by my rules! Now let's finish making history, the right way men. Touch gloves," the referee demanded.

Ringside seats are going berserk. I just witnessed a grown man shed laughter-induced tears. The Timber Man sure does have a way with the crowd. Flash, would you agree?

Absolutely, he's a great referee. I didn't always like having him for my matches, but I love watching fights he officiates.

Why didn't you like it when he was your referee, Flash? I apologize, folks. Where are my manners? I have a very special guest with me ringside for our Third Round: Three Minute Box Talk.

He's one many consider to be the greatest boxer to ever land a punch. The only man in Professional Boxing Association history to retire undefeated winning belts in five different weight classes. He recently retired possessing belts in two weight classes, simultaneously. Flash Shabazz. How's it going, Sport?"

That was rude, and I didn't realize it until you pointed it out. You're a big man for that. Another thing, take this however you want but don't ever call

me, Sport again. I'm a grown man. That's disrespectful. Come correct when you speak to me. My mother is listening.

I apologize. Flash, honestly, I meant no harm.

Apologies aren't necessary. I know that's one of your favorite pet names, for lack of better words, just don't use it with me. To answer your question, he was fair but it's hard staying in the zone when you're trying not to laugh at the referee. He's accidentally funny, yet highly respected. Anytime I heard he was my referee, I'd meditate.

How does meditation help?

It's for mental toughness, Sport. If your opponent catches you slipping for one second, it could be lights out.

I think that's what Tyme is banking on, a lucky punch. What do you think, Flash?

You don't know the man like I do. I wouldn't be surprised if he's putting on a show. He can beat this guy. Melzi was one of the toughest fighters I ever whooped. He's a beast. I've seen him put folks to sleep but I know Tyme can beat him.

So, you're saying he's pretending? Putting on a show just to finish him in four?

You do a great job running with my words. That's just a hunch, I could be wrong.

We shall see as we begin round three. Are you ready, Flash?

Are owls nocturnal?

Last time that I checked.

Of course, I'm ready... Sport.

Round Three

What do you see happening this round, Flash?

75

I see Tyme getting settled in. Manic is on a roll but Tyme has a tough chin. His knees were knocking earlier but I think he has his feet under him now. What about you, Scott?

I see Tyme getting knocked down at the end of the third. I've seen this movie before. Manic is a finisher. He smells blood; that's why I call him the Great White Shark.

Let's see. Here's the bell.

Ding!

Manic comes out firing, connecting with a quick jab and right hook to the head. Tyme Pushes off and glides backwards in a zig-zag pattern.

Uh-oh...

Flash must know something we don't, folks. Stay tuned. Tyme runs up shifting his shoulders in the opposite direction of his previous steps. It's hard to explain folks, but he used it to set up a lighting fast one-two combination. Manic is frozen as Tyme beats his body like a real life punching bag. I haven't seen hands this fast since the man sitting next to me was in the ring.

A big left to body! Jab and a left hook! Followed by a huge right upper cut that sends Manic against the ropes.

Manic is stumbling bad, folks. He's completely lost his center of gravity. Bouncing into a left hand jab to the face, Tyme follows the diversion with a straight right hand. That right hand sent Mavis Melzi through the ropes! I repeat, Mavis Melzi is outside the ring!

"Timber! 1... 2... 3... 4..."

That's what I was afraid of Scott. He did that to a kid from Money, Mississippi when he was thirteen. He calls it Checkmate. He only used it when his best combinations failed. It confuses folk. Makes you wonder what he's doing. Biggest mistake in boxing is watching the fight instead of fighting in it.

People get knocked out of the ring in the amateurs every year. I've never seen anything like this in the Pros and I've seen at least a thousand fights.

Neither have I! He's back on his feet, quickly climbing into the ring. Referee Owens opens the ropes, aiding his reentry.

"Watch your step, Melzi. That's a TKO if you fall.

"5... 6... 7... 8..."

Flash is cracking up in laughter folks.

That's what I'm talking about. That's exactly what I'm talking about. Tyme was in the zone and now he's smirking at Timber Man's comments. Why did he have to say all of that? We know the rules.

Yelling out, 'Timber' all the time doesn't make it any better. Tyme has lost his edge. Watch what I tell you.

Manic enters the ring shaking his head, swinging his arms. Half the front row nearly spilled their drinks. Who would have known dodging boxers would be a reason to spill popcorn on your wife's new dress.

Tyme is too relaxed. Look at his feet, they're flat. He's not fighting on his toes anymore. Timber Man swung the momentum. I know his personality. If I found it funny, it was hilarious to him.

Meeting at center ring with thirty seconds left in the third. Manic is back to slugging it out as the aggressor, attacking Tyme's head and body. Flash, tell us what happened the last time someone got hit with a Checkmate?

The fight was over in the fourth round. The guy never got up. Tyme was down on the scorecards and a knockout was his only way to win in the last round.

Are you saying a knockout is the only way he wins tonight?

I never said that. I think he's going to win this fight whether it's in four like he predicted or if they go the distance to fifteen.

There you have it, folks, straight from the Champ's mouth. But I may be right on my third round knockdown as the Manic continues to pound away on Tyme.

Ten seconds left. Tyme pushes off and fires a couple of jabs followed by another devastating right hook that sends Mavis the Manic stumbling again. This time it's safely to the canvas. Timber Man Owens dives to one knee, start the clock!

"Timber! 1... 2... 3... 4... 5... 6... 7... 8..."

Melzi is up on his feet at four as the bell sounds. You're a natural at this, Flash.

You jiving me, Scott?

No, I am not jiving you. You're a legend in the sport, you make good predictions, you've got personality... That's good stuff, Flash. Can we expect you back on the show?

I appreciate it, Mr. Wilcox. As for coming back, that's up to the people. I don't know if they want to hear from a washed up, old has-been like me.

Washed up? Nonsense, I bet you could go fifteen right now.

Not right now. I eat too many donuts.

I share the same problem. Flash, it's been great having you with us. Thank you for your time, it's been a pleasure. Enjoy the rest of the fight and tell the family I said, hello.

No Problem, Scott. Same to you. Goodnight, everyone.

Flash Shabazz, ladies and gentlemen. He's a Champion, record breaker, and apparently a good friend of the Mighty Mouth. I would've never guessed.

Round Four

In case you're just tuning in folks. You are in for a great one. Manic is down on the score cards thirteen to fourteen. For those of you who may not know, in the PBA, there are three judges who score bouts using either ones or twos.

Winner gets two and the loser of the round gets one. Tyme took the cake after the third with the help of two knockdowns. One of the two was a literal knockout.

Ding!

Round four, people, buckle your seatbelts. Manic looks ready to do work, swinging flurries early. There goes Tyme's hand speed on display again, but on defense. He's punching Melzi's hands.

Tyme circles the ring, moving in and out on his opponent. Manic throws a left jab and right hook to the body. Tyme blocks the body with his left elbow, punching Mavis' other hand with his right hand. This is immaculate timing and hand-eye coordination that we're watching. We'll see how long he keeps it up.

Melzi swings a wild hook Tyme saw coming five minutes ago.

"I hope that's not all you've got!" Rydon shouted.

The Mighty Mouth is back folks!

"You won't land a punch all round!" he warned.

"Shut up," Mavis snarled.

"Make me," Rydon yelled, throwing a punch.

Tyme leans in with a left hand jab.

"Put your hands down," Rydon barked.

Tyme lights him up with back-to-back right hooks.

"It's the fourth round! You know what that means, right?" Rydon asked.

He's bouncing back again. Here comes a third Poster Punch! Wait, he's still going! Tyme is going for the knockout. Manic has lost it! He's swinging at anything.

Tyme jumps to a halt, fainting with a right hook. Manic is shaken, he blocked an invisible punch! What a huge left hook by Tyme! Owens hits the deck to start the count for a third time!

Timber! "1... 2... 3... 4... 5... 6... 7... 8... 9... 10! He's done!"

What a fight! We're sending you to the ring now. Stay tuned for our exclusive interview with THE Rydon Tyme!

"Thank you for coming out, Detroit. You were great all night. Give yourselves a hand," the fight promoter said, praising the crowd.

"Tonight's contest ended in the fourth round by way of knockout. Your *new* Number One Contender, *Highland Park's Finest*, Rydon Tyme!" Jo shouted, passing the microphone to Rydon.

"When did I say I was going to drop him!?" Rydon asked the sold-out crowd.

"The fourth round!" they all shouted.

"When!?"

"IN THE FOURTH ROUND!" they cheered.

"Thank you for coming out! Drive safely," Rydon said, blowing a kiss to the crowd.

After a brief conversation with Referee Owens, Rydon left the four corners to fulfill his post-fight interview as agreed upon contractually.

Ladies and Gentlemen, I have a young boxer with me to my left, who may be taking over the sport. He's undefeated winning both fights by knockout. His hands move at speeds I've never seen before. A boxer way ahead of his time. Welcome to the show, Rydon Tyme.

It's good to be here, only because I get to talk to the people. Not because I'm next to you.

Talk about first impressions. What's that supposed to mean, Tyme? I'm a fan of yours.

You're a poser. Flash told me everything you said about me and how you thought I'd fall at the end of the third.

When did you talk to Flash? The fight just ended.

He came to my corner. We grew up together. You didn't think he would tell me? That's the only reason I agreed to do the interview because I wanted to thank you.

You wanted to thank me?

Yes, sir. You ended this fight a lot earlier than I thought. I had him figured out in the second round. He was amazing in the first. One of the best fighters I've ever faced but he never changed anything. It was the same ole song. Charge, punch, punch, charge. I'm a quick learner. I was out of moves by the third round, so I created new ones.

I'm glad I could help out. Speaking of the third, you sent him through the ropes. Flash said this has happened before. Tell us about it?

I was thirteen the first time it happened. I was doing a little talking in the ring...

You don't say.

I thought you asked me a question, Scott?

I did.

Then let me finish the story. We were going at it all fight. He beat me up badly in the first two rounds. I came back in the third and dropped him in the fourth. Same as tonight! Déjà vu. You should feel bad doubting me the way you did, Wilcox! I hope you listen next time I say something. It will make you sound like you know what you're talking about for once.

Easy, easy. I'm sorry!

Relax, Scott. This is mild for me. I'm just direct. How did I do tonight?

I thought you did ok. I don't know much about you, yet. I'm still feeling you out. You proved you can take a punch; you're resilient. Like Dave Sampson, are you familiar with him?

Of course, he was my father's favorite boxer.

You have power and some of the fastest hands in the world. Defense needs work, but you showed in the fourth how to revolutionize the way people defend punches. I've never seen someone defend so many punches that way. If I were a teacher, I'd give you a B-. Your corner could have saved you some wear and tear if you listened to them early in the fight.

That's a fair assessment from the outside looking in. The first round was his, I give him that. In the second round, I had to prove to myself that I could take his punches. When my knees started shaking, half was my nerves and the other half I was in a daze.

I haven't felt like that in a long time. I needed the peace of mind for myself. I've been hit harder. A kid named Ty Farmer hits harder than anyone I ever faced. But that's the hardest I've been hit in front of fifty thousand people before. He didn't stand a chance once I got used to having all eyes on me in the third and fourth rounds.

Now I understand. Flash said he thought you were putting on a show so you could drop him in the fourth.

Flash always thinks I'm up to something. Half the time, he over analyzes things about me.

Hey, Tyme, I have a question?

That's why I'm here.

What do you think about the nicknames I gave you?

I like the Mighty Mouth believe it or not. That's the only one I've heard.

What about the Steel Chin? Especially after tonight's fight.

I don't know about that one. It sounds like I get hit a lot. It may have to grow on me. Use it creatively. While I'm thinking about it, I'm focusing on defense for my next fight in September, just for you.

Do you have an opponent yet?

It'll be you if I keep hearing about you doubting me. It's been good talking, but I have to get going. I have a date with the Mrs. tonight. We're taking a vacation in the morning.

Love is a beautiful thing, isn't it? Where to?

Very true. I'm not sure yet. I'll find out when I get home. Thanks for having me, Scott. Goodnight, folks out there in radio land! Be great in all that you do.

```
            Paris, France
            Eiffel Tower
             3:45PM GMT
        1959 May 11, Monday
```

"Unbelievable."

Gabriella was speechless as they turned down the lustful lanes of the Paris streets, admiring all the boutiques they drove past. "Ooh let's go over by the water," she suggested, pointing from the backseat window.

A lot of things changed since Rydon became the Professional Boxing Association's brightest star. There were many perks associated with his new title as the Number One Contender.

Such as the jet-black limousine and chauffeur service courtesy of the company. "You can drop us off up here, sir," Rydon instructed to the driver.

"Yes, sir. Will do. Take this. Press the button when you're ready and it will send your location to this Direction Box, and I'll be able to find you," the driver said, having been separated for the first time.

"This can do all of that?" Rydon asked with fascination.

"Old man Grove never stops working."

"Don't I know it. What does the Direction Box do?"

Gabriella sat back catching a funk. She was overly anxious to explore the town and Rydon was busy being a nerd. Looking out the window, she already planned their first three stops while he made a new friend.

"Arrows light up on this here black screen. It'll be up, down, left, or right. If it flashes, that means we're within twenty yards of each other. It shows direction too. North, south, east, and west but it only shows the first letter. The screen isn't big enough for the whole word I guess," the driver stated.

Bored beyond belief, the men's conversations was lasting forever. Gabriella took measures in her own hands, giving hints to wrap it up. Hooking her arm around Rydon's was her first step.

Sitting back for comfort, Rydon wanted to know more. "Is this a speaker?"

"Yea, it lets me tell you where I am. Watch this," the driver said, pressing the button to the microphone.

Hey, I'm here. Do you see me?

Seeing it may take a while, Gabriella got comfortable resting her elbow on the door ledge. With her hand holding her chin, she closed her eyes as a last resort to get Rydon's attention.

"That's out of sight! How far does this thing reach?" Rydon asked, ignorant to it all.

"I can find you anywhere within twenty miles."

"Wow, is it waterproof?"

"I don't know about that. I think your wife fell asleep though, sir." The driver nodded in Gabriella's direction.

Waking her with a kiss on the cheek, Gabriella blushed for multiple reasons.

"Wake up lady, we have places to go and people to dodge. I mean, people to see," Rydon said with a smile.

The driver opened the door for them as they exited the vehicle, standing on the corner looking like true tourists. With their eyes to the sky as if waiting for a miracle, the couple tried their best finding the top of the massive structure ahead of them.

"Are we going to the top of the Eiffel Tower or are we taking the boat ride first?" Rydon asked, ready to make a move.

Standing on the corner, sporting a money green tam, spotless white shirt, and a matching smile, the camera hanging from his neck was screaming for a photo shoot.

"Excuse me, miss, could you take a picture of my wife and me?" Rydon asked of another tourist nearby.

"Absolutely, I love, love, love you two together. You look so in love." The old lady smiled.

"Thank you," he said, smiling with his head bowed.

"Smile," she prompted, as they posed for the picture.

"Let's take the boat, get off on the other side then I'll let you carry me upstairs," he offered.

"Man, please, but now that you mention it, I might have to get on your back. That's a long way to the top."

"Tell me about it," Rydon said, shadowboxing with himself.

Gabriella continued to watch her prize fighter embrace his role as People's Champ, while a group of tourists gathered for the one-man show.

" *Voila lui, la Puissant Bouche!*" a boy shouted, grabbing his father's backpack as his ice cream fell to the sun kissed grass.

"Baby what's Puissant Bouche mean?" Rydon asked in a soft tone to his running mate.

"Mighty Mouth, why?" Gabriella answered.

"We have to get out of here soon or we'll get spotted and miss the boat. Little man over there just called me Mighty Mouth." Rydon nodded while they speed walked away.

On their way to the water, Rydon noticed another child stuck in awe. His soccer ball had gotten away from him when he noticed the star. "Here you go Mr. Sir," he said to the boy.

As he dribbled the ball to the young man, Rydon shook his hand before the Tyme's slipped away. Right on time to board the boat preparing to leave the pier.

"Mr. International! You go, boy," Gabriella whispered with a kiss to the lips having witnessed it all. Making room underneath his muscular arms, she fell into a trance, absorbing everything that surrounded her.

86

```
Highland Park, Michigan
Paradise Condominiums, Manchester Street
5:02AM Eastern Standard Time
1959 November 30, Monday
```

In the passing months, Rydon Tyme put together a string of victories that landed him a spot in the title bout. His gaps between fights grew thinner and thinner because they never went the distance or close to it.

Beating the best the business had to offer, there was little doubt in anyone's mind that things would be any different whenever he got his shot at the title.

"Hello?"

"Wake up, Don. We have to talk. Meet us at the gym at five minutes to six."

"What's up?"

"You don't want to know. See you in a little bit," Jo said, hanging up the phone.

Stepping out of bed, Jo's call made Rydon feel uneasy about what to expect. The last time Jo summoned him to a meeting at the spur of the moment, he was recruited and offered a boxing contract.

Kissing his sleeping wife on the cheek, her body said what her lips couldn't, as she repositioned herself for better comfort. Finishing his early morning routine, Rydon pulled the strings to his hooded sweatshirt and laced his boots before his early morning departure.

After a ten minute warmup run to *The Bag*, he entered the dark gym in search of his comrades.

"We're up here, Don," Jo called from the upstairs office.

Rydon's sense of belonging made it easy to grow used to the newspaper clippings, feature articles, and awards bearing his name, leading to the top step. Entering the only room in the building emitting light, he got straight to business.

"I ask for one day a week to come in after noon but instead, my phone rings at five in the morning."

"Same ole, Donny. I told Jo you would cut into him about that. Relax, have a seat," Marcel said, motioning to the seating area.

Taking a load off in the Thinking Man recliner, Rydon kicked his feet up for a meeting he could see going longer than expected.

"I know you're going to have a lot of questions and might get disappointed but let me finish speaking first." Taking a sip of orange juice, Marcel licked his lips to prepare for a long first round. "Are you thirsty?" he asked.

"Water but quit stalling, Cel. I'm still supposed to be in REM sleep right about now," Rydon answered.

"Long story short, the title fight is going to be in Vidor next month on the twenty-sixth, not downtown Detroit in July. After Flash retired last year, the titles were vacated. You were Melzi's ninth fight. He was two away from ten straight wins and a spot in the title fight with Chris Conner. Conner was ranked third. When Flash retired, he moved up a spot."

Rydon possessed the ability to suppress his emotions which made him unreadable at times. His face hid his broken heart at the sound of the news, but he refused to let it show. It wasn't his style.

"Well, apparently the Journeyman hates you with a passion. He's been a different fighter since you last saw him. He's slimmer, faster, and looks thirty all over again. I know you don't pay attention to the media, but he hasn't lost a fight since he fought you and none of his fights have gone past the fifth round."

On the verge of interrupting what sounded like rambled, mumbo-jumbo, Rydon bit his tongue at a break in the story. "There's a clause in the PBA bylaws that says, anytime a Number One Contender and a second ranked boxer fights while the title is vacated, then that match becomes the championship fight.

"Two belts are on the line. The PBA heavyweight title and the LOTT Magazine belt for the man who beat the man. Since we agreed to the rematch back in April, it's nothing we can do. What it really boils down to after Connor's loss Saturday night is, you're the number one contender and the Journeyman is now number two," Marcel said as he sipped his orange juice. "Your title fight has been moved up seven months," he said, shrugging.

"And relocated," Rydon barked back.

```
Highland Park, Michigan
15900 Woodward Avenue
11:07AM Eastern Standard Time
1959 December 19, Saturday
```

Making their way to a basketball game at the Highland Park City High School gymnasium, Gabriella and Rydon trickled in minutes before tipoff with the other fans in attendance. Now accustomed to being the main attraction, chatter ceased when all eyes shifted their way.

"Not this again," Rydon whispered in Gabriella's ear with a kiss to the cheek, pretending to be oblivious to it all. The second their bottoms touched the bleacher seats, flashes from cameras reflected off the freshly waxed floor like a mirror.

"Don't worry, honey, look," she said, pointing to the boys in front of them who had just stepped foot on the court, preparing for the national anthem. "The flashing lights were for them, not us."

The distinct sound of Rydon's laugh in a silent room, shifted the attention he was able to avoid directly toward him.

Let's have a huge round of applause for HP's Finest and the Professional Boxing Association's Number One Contender, the Chosen Dreamer, Rydon Tyme!

A lengthy applause rang across the court as the boys acknowledged Rydon by jumping in the air, pumping their fist as if they already won.

Please rise for the singing of the National Anthem.

O say can you see, by the dawn's early light.
What so proudly we hailed at the twilight last gleaming,
Whose broad stripes and bright stars through the perilous fight,
O'er the ramparts we watched, were so gallantly streaming.
And the rockets' red glare, the bombs bursting in air,
Gave proof through the night that our flag was still there.
O say does that star spangled banner yet wave.
O'er the land and of the free,
And the home,
Of the,
Brave...

Let's hear it for the boys Polar Bear, varsity basketball team!

You better wake up and show your love! We know it's early, but this is the Brother City Holiday Classic. You better bring it!

The stands rumbled with excitement. Whenever the Polar Bears played well, it resurrected the spirit of the city. Everybody had something to say anytime the boys put together a win streak. Eleven and counting was the most recent.

"And now, the starting lineup for YOUR Highland Park Polar Bears!"

H-P!
H-P!
H-P!

The crowd chanted with the boys.

At center, the big man in the paint, some call him Tank because he's built like one. Standing six, nine from the floor, big ole Ken Moore!

The crowd went wild over one of the best athletes the school had ever seen. He played three sports, earning first team Mighty Michigan honors across the board. Scouts traveled from all over the country to watch Ken play in the tournament, being one of the country's most polished big men.

Every December, the city hosted a four team tournament with schools being represented from across the state. The winner of the competition earned an early bid in the high school National Championship Tournament.

The crowd roared for player after player making their way off the bench and onto the hardwood. Ready for another event sure to leave them standing, most of the loudest cheers came during player introductions.

A starting five filled with graduating seniors, the floor general was everything but.

At point guard, six feet and still growing, a year removed from his middle school prom... the Freshman Phenom, Mr. 'Let's have some fun', Bobby Hamp-ton!

High school basketball in the City School League always left the people wanting more. CSL prospects played with a different swagger than its competition. For the Polar Bears, their lack of local media coverage put a chip on their shoulder.

"Bring it in, fellas. All season, we've talked about how much folks doubt us. We came too far and screamed too loud, telling folks we're for real. Well, it looks like they listened! I never seen so many people at any of our games before," Bobby shouted, putting his arm around the shoulders of the twin brothers, a small and power forward, forming a circle at half court.

No one made a fuss when Bobby Hampton was named team captain. He was a natural-born leader. A man trapped inside a boy's body, mature well beyond his years. His vocal presence in the locker room changed the entire culture in a single preseason.

A roster of individuals turned into a band of brothers, chasing after a state title. "After Big Ken wins the tip, leave everything in you right here on this floor," he said, gaining momentum while pointing to their logo at midcourt. "No regrets. If it feels like a good shot, take it. If coach pulls you for it, I'll tell him it was my call. As long as we win this tournament.

"We brought everybody out, the mayors of the Brother Cities, our girlfriends, Donny and Gabby. Rydon Tyme is in the building! He's supposed to be training but he's here to watch us play. That's his number seven jersey up there in the rafter's. We can't let the city down, not tonight. Pose soire! We have a long day ahead of us, fellas. Nobody wins in our house, but us. Let's have some fun!

"Hands in, hands in. *HP one hundred* on three," Bobby instructed.

"One, two, three... HP!"

"One hundred!"

The boys stagger chanted as they broke the huddle. The floor shook beneath them, with the fans echoing their call.

"These boys came to play today; you can see it in their eyes," Rydon said, holding his arms around Gabriella who sat between his legs one bleacher lower.

Before halftime, word spread of Rydon's arrival. Reporters in the area had first dibs while others across the country could only hope he wouldn't leave before they touched down.

"Tyme, do you have time for an interview? Jessie Winters, Hamtramck Review?" a reporter asked.

"Nope, none. Watch the game. That's the real story," he said, dismissing the request. "Let's go, Big Ken!" Rydon shouted from his seat.

More bright lights blinded him from the main attraction. "The story is this way!" Rydon yelled, pointing towards the court as Bobby Hampton threaded the needle through traffic to a streaking Ken Moore.

The Polar Bears traded baskets all game long with the Detroit Prep School Panthers. "Timeout!" Coach Trunnel said, followed by a whistle from across the floor, micromanaging the teams last thirteen seconds.

"Tie game. We have nothing to lose. We either win now or in overtime," Coach Trunnel informed the team. "Bobby, at the ten second mark, kick it to Samuels in the right corner.

"Samuels, after you get the ball from Bobby, run to the top of the key. Nathaniel, spot up on the left corner like you're looking for a shot. When Samuels gets to the top of the key, run to the right corner and make the shot.

"Yes, coach!" Samuels replied.

"Bring it in. Champs on three. One, two, three!" Coach Trunnel directed.

"Champs!" With the extra boost from the fans, the ground shook their feet once again.

Nathaniel received his cue from Samuels and caught the ball in the right corner with his feet pivoted. His hands palmed the ball, releasing a beautifully arched shot that snapped the nets as the buzzer blared in the background. Over seven hundred people already on their feet, went wild and rushed the court to celebrate with the team.

The boys tackled the unsung hero in the corner of the court, while the news cameras snapped more pictures than a family reunion. The dogpile on the hardwood gave Rydon and Gabriella the prime opportunity to sneak out for lunch. The championship game was set for two hours later after the battle for third place.

Walking into another sellout game, Rydon and Gabriella headed up the bleachers, all the way to the top center section. The couple found a spot behind good friends of the family. "Ruby, you look beautiful as always," Gabriella said, kissing the woman's cheek.

"Ray, how's business going?" Rydon asked, shaking hands with the gentleman.

"It's going great. Junior runs the Woodward and Seven Mile store on weekends. That's him there, number five," Ray said, bragging on his firstborn son.

"That was a mean growth spurt. How tall is he now?"

"Six-two, sixteen years old. He'll get another one before his senior year, wait and see. He's the sixth man now but he might be taking Frank Tyson's spot."

"Because he's a freshman? We started B Hamp all season. I still can't believe Frank Tyson chose the Generals," Rydon questioned in a deflated tone and matching body language. "Over the Highland Park Polar Bears," Rydon said, gloating as he popped the school's logo on his varsity jacket.

"B Hamp and Frank Tyson had to split, I guess? It would've been too easy if they played together after going undefeated in middle school."

"Keep dreaming. The Polar Bears never had a chance. He comes from a long line of Generals. It's in the boy's bloodline, his DNA," Ray insisted. "He shot up this summer too. Seven inches, he's my height now."

"How tall are you?"

"Six-seven. They're transitioning him into a big man."

"You know what, I saw this big kid wearing number three and it didn't even register that was Frank Tyson. I figured he must've switched numbers this year. That's unbelievable. You ought to advise them not to try that experiment against us. Ken Moore is for real.

"I know that's not little Zeek, is it?" Rydon asked, distracted by the little guy sitting between his parents.

"Yep." The little boy smiled with a missing tooth.

"How old are you now, Isaiah," Rydon asked in wonderment.

"Eight, going on nine." Isaiah grinned.

"Eight, going on nine!? You need a job, little dude," Rydon joked with the group. I saw your little brother at the Honor Roll Rally, but I didn't see you. How's school?" Rydon questioned.

"Good," Little Isaiah dragged out, leaning back in his seat and out of sight.

"Where is Young Paul?"

"With his grandparents, toy shopping. Then probably out for ice cream and whatever else he wants to do, I'm sure," Ruby thought aloud, shaking her head.

As the old friends caught up on the past, the Revere High School Generals were ready for war. Being a basketball powerhouse for over two decades, current players were used to the spotlight. Many of them transferred there solely for their reputable math department and well coached basketball program.

State championships weren't aspirations, they were expectations. "Atten-tion... hut!" one young man called out.

Hut, 2, 3, 4... Hut, 2, 3, 4...

The boys kept the cadence, slapping their jersey covered thighs while removing warm up gear, one by one in a rhythmic motion.

Atten-tion... Hut!

SALUTE!

The crowd screamed, finishing off a pregame ritual that ended without lights. A loud boom followed by steam and spotlights launched the five starters to the forefront.

"Salute!" Ray yelled, standing to his feet, clapping his hands. "Now that's an introduction!" he shouted as a proud alumni and MVP of the 1939 National Championship Tournament team.

"Hey, keep it down, Ray. Somebody might hear you. You're wearing the wrong school colors to be so loud," Rydon spoke confidently. "Go Polar Bears!"

"Speaking of school colors, Gabriella was a General before she put on the blue and white. Her jump shot was nothing to play with." Ray laughed, wearing his blue and gold varsity sweater and matching rope chain.

"I told Ry I'm torn for this one. I love both schools, I can't pick. He keeps telling me, 'That's good and all but remember what your diploma says.' Gabriella informed the other Generals in attendance, mocking Rydon's deep voice and dramatic gestures.

"You tell him, girl. You won a state title with both schools, you should be torn," Ruby added, joining in on the fun. "Her letterman is even half Polar Bears and half Generals."

"I guess," Rydon said in defeat.

"Thank you, Ruby. It's not my fault HP was the closest school with a golf team. I missed the greens."

"Two and a half Generals to one and a half Polar Bears, this is going to be a long game. I can see it now," Rydon said, shaking his head.

Press coverage was very sketchy throughout the Brother Cities of Detroit and Highland Park. Prep schools in the city had a much better chance receiving televised game coverage or being mentioned in the newspaper than their crosstown adversaries.

Parents of the students often allied and pooled resources to ensure a stable future for student athletes, helping them pay college tuition as walk-ons. Very few schools in the Brother Cities drew attention from the media. The Revere High School Generals were one of them.

Winning seven of the last eleven state titles, the press they received was similar to the Professional Basketball League's Detroit Fire.

With the clock winding down on pregame warmups, reporters began searching the court for interviews. Halting his search at midcourt, Burt Rapids from DAC News 43 darted up the stairs. "Here they come again. I'm about to set them straight, my lady. Excuse me." Rising to his feet, Rydon was ready to lash out at any media member who invaded his privacy.

"Radiator Ray, we miss watching you warm up that jump shot before tipoff. Is it ok to ask you a few questions," Burt asked Ray, initiating a pregame interview.

"Of course, how's the family?" Ray asked the reporter.

Left in an awkward position, Rydon grabbed Gabriella's hand to follow him to the exit at the top of the bleachers. Going with the flow of it all, she slipped out behind him. Up the bleacher stairs and out the door they went.

Like clockwork, Rydon was always spotted by his closest observers. "Detective Tyme!" A young girl pointed using the only hand she had available with a mouth full of crushed caramel apples.

Waving at the little one, Rydon pushed the glass door to the right of them. The east stairwell exit led them to a concession stand with very few people in line. "Baby, you know I'm always ready to ride but a couple times, you blew your own cover." Gabriella giggled.

"I know. I have to trust this new haircut and no sideburns look."

"I like them both," she replied, picking a piece of lint from his chin hairs.

Returning to their seats in time for tip off, the fans cheered emphatically as Frank Tyson and Ken Moore approached midcourt. Ken Moore hopped around, preparing for the jump ball while the shot clock sounded to conclude pregame warmups.

"He jumps higher than anybody I've ever seen his size. We used to call those springs or bunnies when I was growing up," Rydon said to his counterpart after the jump ball.

"I know, Rydon," Gabriella replied, glued to the game.

"Just making sure. I heard one youngsta call them hops the other day. I love it when you call me Rydon too by the way. Say it again."

"Ry-don," she said, turning towards him, slowly biting her lip.

"You're going to get me in trouble," he responded, kissing her forehead. Camera flashes burst on que, freezing the moment in history.

"With who?" Gabriella teased.

"Them," Rydon replied, nodding at photographers and media members.

"So?" she dismissed nonchalantly.

Spending the last few hours on the run avoiding cameras and large crowds of people left Rydon exhausted. Switching his routine to train at night for the title fight was a bittersweet experiment. Although the games had concluded, Rydon's workday was just getting started.

"We did it. You managed to get away without a single interview," Gabriella said, sneaking a kiss between steps.

A flashing light in front of them left Rydon shaking his head. "Spoke too soon. The one time I think we can walk down the stairwell like everybody else, this happens." Waiting in the lobby between the stairs and the gymnasium entrance for his arrival was a sea of reporters and cameramen.

"Tyme, can we have an interview? Titus Attucks, Highland Park Sun."

"Of course, brother. Good to see you again. Let's talk," Rydon agreed, shaking his hand.

"Thanks, sir. What are you doing here?" Titus inquired.

"I came to watch the boys play. They were talking about closing down the school for good and I've been here all week to see that it doesn't happen. I wouldn't be where I am without this place. Those boys on the court and all the students in the stands showed it's a lot of life left in this building."

"You said you've been here all week, are you on the school's Executive Board?"

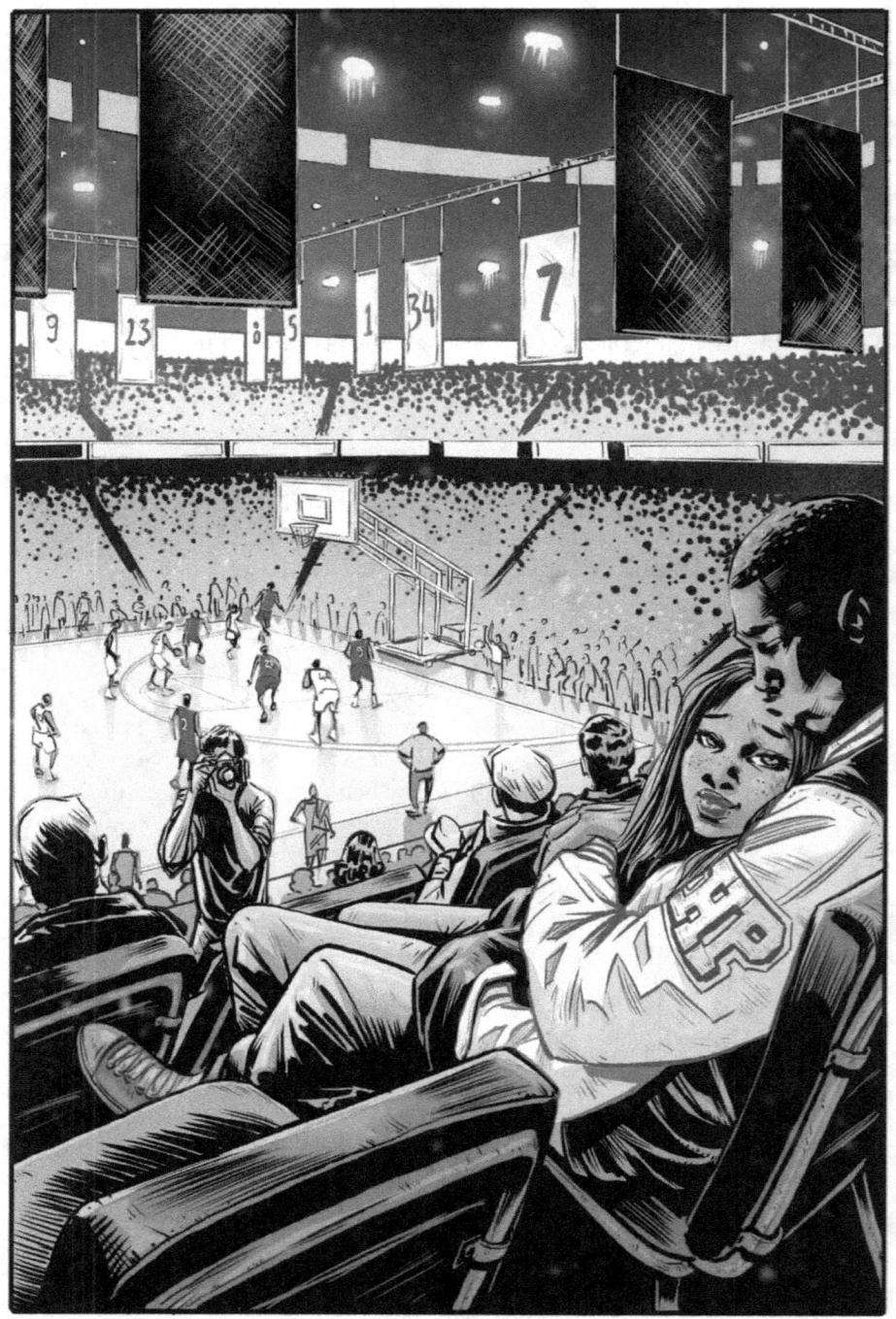

"My wife and I are on the donors list. This was scheduled to be the school's last year open because the building is so old. It's falling apart."

"Is it going to stay open?"

"I'm sure of it. The school was able to raise one hundred thousand dollars. Renovations start over winter break. The school will look completely different in the new year."

"Solid," the reporter said with his fist balled. "About the fight, any predictions?"

"You know what, Mr. Attucks, I know when he's going down, but I won't cheat the people. I want you all to be surprised for once since this is my last fight."

"Last fight? Jeb Carter. Erie, Michigan Review," he stated, giving his credentials.

"Excuse me, we're having a conversation. I'll open the floor in a few minutes. Hang on," Rydon said, halting the man with the palm of his hand.

"This is your last fight this year?" Titus asked, seeking clarity.

"I'm retiring after the Venom in Vidor. This is your story. Get it to the people this evening. The game just ended. You can beat traffic if you leave now."

Finishing a private interview a few feet away with a new ally, Rydon gave Titus the breaking news before the others and sent him on his way. "ASAP, Mr. Attucks," he reminded him.

"Yes, sir," Titus agreed, running off to his car.

While Titus went to write the future, Rydon was stuck in the present. "Ok, folks, we have a half hour together. I know I say this at the beginning of every press conference but *please* be creative."

"Hey, Tyme, Lenny Colbert, independent reporter. Two questions. What's your beef with us? We're just trying to make a living. Our job is to ask the questions folks at home are screaming at their television sets," Lenny concluded.

"I second that," Jeb said as the group agreed.

"My other question is, what's this we hear about the Venom in Vidor being your last fight?" Lenny asked, demanding answers.

"Let's tackle the first question. Ever since I was a kid, I've seen the media slander the names of good, hardworking folks. My grandfather used to always tell me, 'If you don't like something, change it.' So, when I went to law school, I was also working on a Master's in Journalism.

"Everything, not *everything* that's an overstatement. Too much of what I read in the paper goes against everything I learned in school. If someone on McNichols commits a crime, they're a thug and a menace. But if someone commits that same crime on Thirteen Mile, they're misunderstood. If anyone is misunderstood, it's the man on Six Mile!" Rydon shouted, pointing his finger to the crowd.

Taking the words right out his mouth, "Go ahead," was all one bystander could say.

"I know some of you are getting paid under the table to twist stories, just like I know about there being crooked cops in the system. The same way I'm cleaning the precincts... I'm cleaning the presses. My mentor would call it, *writing without ink.* That's what they say when you let folks control what you write.

Pens tattooed notepads in lightening speeds, as spectators finally started to figure out what was going on. "When I find folks who report the news for the right reasons, I offer them a career. You interested?"

"Sure!" Lenny shouted, pointing with his pen.

"Meet me at the Sun, tomorrow at noon. Yes, the Venom in Vidor will be my last fight. I signed up to win a championship belt and leave in good health. I'm in the best shape of my life and this time next week, I'll be heavyweight champion of the world," Rydon promised, shadow boxing as usual.

"Gus Sparks, Birmingham Beat. Are you ready for your last dance in Texas? Hope you don't think the jewelry man can save you down there. They gon' catch you out after dark in Vidor, boy. Maybe even tonight," the reporter said with a thick southern accent.

"Is that a threat? Grab him!" Rydon commanded, as seven men scattered throughout the crowd, restrained the reporter.

"Take my keys. You know where to go." Rydon said, removing the badge underneath his shirt for the first time in months, before kissing Gabriella goodbye.

```
                    Vidor, Texas
                Texas State Airport
            4:13AM Central Standard Time
            1959 December 23, Wednesday
```

Days away from the biggest fight of his life, both in and out of the ring, Rydon was ready for whatever. Stepping down the brightly lit stairs of the Boeing 720, Gabriella wiped her sleepy eyes and grabbed hold to Rydon's left arm.

From baggage claim to the car rental service desk, Rydon could feel Gabriella's grip getting tighter. "Everything alright down there?" he asked, sensing her discomfort.

"You know what's wrong. They act like they've never seen black folks before," Gabriella said, catching an attitude with the attendant who hassled Rydon since their introduction.

"If I were you, I'd watch what I say. This isn't Michigan, ma'am," the attendant said, with a tongue sharp enough to shave steel.

"Well, if you were me, you'd have more class. But if you want to take it there, I'll show you how we do it up north. I'm from Detroit, sweetheart, show some respect," Gabriella said, flipping the hair covering her face.

Left, right, left, right, left, right went Rydon's pupils as he tried finding a gap in the verbal dispute to deescalate the situation.

"Just give us the keys, Mary. With a name like that, you'd think you would have some honor."

Blinking wildly, Rydon followed the arm leading him to the parking lot. "I know how much you love and respect women, Ry; but you can't let them talk to you any kind of way just because they have estrogen," Gabriella said, scolding her husband.

"*This doesn't look like you. Why do you deserve a limo? You, box?* That was just plain rude!" she went on, bolting to the car.

"It was funny to me. I was about to laugh in her face until I heard you snap on her. Blatant racism is comical to me. I always think, *one day* they'll hear how goofy it all sounds."

"I hear you, Beany, I do. But I'm your wife and if I don't disrespect you, they *can't* disrespect you. Deal?" she proposed, extending her pinky finger.

"Here you go waving that baby carrot of yours around again. Deal," he said, sealing the agreement with a kiss. "Here's the key to the Penthouse in case I forget to give it to you later."

"Penthouse?" Gabriella said, raising her eyebrow.

"Yup. The PBA treats their boxers like kings, sweetie. And here comes the limo. I requested our same driver from Paris."

"I see," she said nodding in approval. "That was your pal," Gabriella said as she snickered.

"Madam, Monsieur," the driver said, opening the door to the 1960 Pentagon Enchantment in front of the Texas State Airport. Entering the backseat of the extended automobile changed their scenery but not their perception.

"Did you see how those people looked at us when he opened the door?"

"Like somebody smeared limburger cheese on their top lip?" Rydon answered.

"Of all things, you are so funny. I'll be glad when this Civil Rights War is over, and folks start acting their age again," Gabriella said with a pout, gazing out the window.

"Don't hold your breath," Rydon warned. "At this pace, it won't end until sometime in the twenty-first century."

"Racism in the two thousands? I don't believe it. It'll be long gone by then. No one is that stubborn." Gabriella laughed, slapping Rydon's arm. "You're so silly."

```
Vidor, Texas
Shine Jewelry and Loans
10:00AM Central Standard Time
1959 December 23, Wednesday
```

Since becoming a professional boxer, Rydon's appearance drastically changed. The infamous detective was making people forget about his life before boxing because of how much success he was having in the ring.

Everything started with his style. He had to look the part as the sport's top star. Rydon began wearing more suits, sweaters, and his favorite of them all, silk. The only thing left to do was to shine bright like a diamond.

Entering the jewelry store, Rydon held the attention of the room as if he had been crowned Man of the Year. His swagger captivated customers like a moving speech, with one person looking a bit intimidated and unsure of what to do.

"George, you don't look so happy to see me," Rydon said, removing his sunglasses.

"No, sir, I am," George replied quickly.

"Do you have the package I asked you for?"

"Nine gold Linx watches; seven men's, one young adult and one for women. Seven gold rope chains with customized seven pendants. I also have this for you as a token of my appreciation."

George Hamlet reached into the glass display and pulled out a case wrapped in cloth. Revealing a handcrafted jewelry box, George removed a silver timepiece.

"Since your name is Tyme, here's a little clock," he said with a shrug.

Rydon looked at the man as if he heard a bad joke until he picked up the equipment and held it in his hands. The cold, round metal fit perfectly into his palm like a ripe mandarin orange.

"This is beautiful. My grandfather had a gold one similar to this many years ago. Thank you," Rydon said, while he traced the patterns with his fingers. "Do you have the other things I requested?"

Looking as if he didn't want to cooperate, George led Rydon to the back office of the jewelry store. The stench from the room made it an unpleasant experience for Rydon.

"What's that smell?" Rydon ask with his nose scrunched.

"Sometimes I don't get home, so I sleep here. Things get busy during the week. Once, I stayed from Monday to Monday."

"Do you bathe? It smells awful back here," Rydon said, waving and fanning his nose. "Get a life, G."

Embarrassed by his surroundings, George moved quickly, sorting and gathering things on his desk. "I know it's here somewhere," he said, rifling through the papers scattered across his desk.

"This is pathetic, George. No grown man should live so savage." Rydon frowned.

"It's not as bad as it looks. I know where everything is; it's organized chaos," George said, wiping sweat from his forehead.

After thumbing through dozens of papers, he finally found what he was looking for. "Here it is," he said, holding a red folder in his hand.

"Good deal. Thanks again for the gifts," Rydon said, slapping the man on the back with a heavy hand.

Shortly after leaving the jewelry store, Rydon made his way to the gym for his last practice before the fight. "Is this where we're training?" he asked, entering the facility. "They show us no respect!"

Over the last year, Rydon's life took a drastic turn. One call on New Year's Eve resulted in a career change. In that span, he grew used to the lavish lifestyle of a PBA Boxer. In each of his previous fights, Rydon sparred in state-of-the-art training facilities stocked with the most up to date equipment. His current setting was everything but.

"Are you seeing what I'm seeing, Marcel, Jo?" Rydon said, reaching for what was left of the speed bag that had detached from the swinging hook above it. Shaking his head, Rydon looked inside the heavy bag next to it, pulling its stuffing out.

"I don't know what to say right now," Marcel mumbled with his head hung. "Look at the ring," he said, pointing to eight mattresses that formed a square in the center of the cemented floor.

"Jefferson's camp booked this place," Jo answered.

PBA fight promoters were responsible for arranging training facilities. In most cases, promoters had their reputations on the line and saw that they provided only the best services. In this particular case, they couldn't care less.

"Y'all see the Journeyman sponsored his own fight? He's never sponsored his own fight. How'd he get enough money to sponsor a title fight?" Rydon asked.

"A lot of people hate you, Don. You haven't realized that yet? He had people throwing money at him for the rematch after the fight in the city," Jo said, catching Rydon up to speed.

"They hate me, what for?" Rydon asked, oblivious to it all.

"You're too real and you don't have a filter," Jo enlightened him.

"Too real, what does that even mean? And what do you mean I don't have a filter? I'm the mild one. You're worse than me!" Rydon stated with confusion.

"Mild!? You thumped a grown man in the middle of the forehead earlier this year," Jo countered. "Besides, this isn't about me because I'm not the superstar, you are. The point is, you're loud. They can't control you and you're fearless.

"They, whoever *they* are, can't handle influential orators because it becomes an issue when you have fans and little kids pretending to be you. You're a superstar, Don and after you weather the storm, you'll be a champion in less than a week."

Stepping back to look at the situation, Rydon could see where Jo was coming from but even still, he needed answers.

"I guess I'll just spar in a warehouse that smells like George's office. I have no jump ropes. I *think* this is a medicine ball," Rydon said, criticizing everything he pulled out of the equipment bag. "Listen to me. We did more with much less back in the day," he reminded himself as Jo and Marcel agreed, mid flashback.

Rounding the barn eleven times, Rydon's mile run was just what he needed to warm up before releasing more frustration on the poorly taped heavy bag. "This bag is awful. It won't last through one of our practices," Marcel said, jabbing at the bag.

"Grab a headgear, Marcel. You said you'd spar with me when the time was right. This is my last practice and don't tell me you're retired because it didn't stop Flash from suiting up a few weeks ago," Rydon reminded him.

"Do you remember what happened the last time we boxed?"

"We were seven years old, Marcelo," Rydon said, straight-faced.

"Marcelo!" Jo laughed. "I haven't heard your full name in years."

"That wasn't the question," Marcel said, pausing dramatically. "The question was, do you remember who was the only person to drop the Mighty Mouth? *That's* the question!"

"You were, but I still won on every judge's scorecard. After you got a twenty count," Rydon reasoned, chuckling at his own snap back.

"You sure? I thought it was a split. Either way, the ref said eight. So, it was eight. Lucky punch," Marcel shrugged.

"Fellas," Jo interrupted. "Grow up and handle this like men." He tossed two sacks stuffed with gloves, headgear, shoes, t-shirts, and trunks to the ground, atop the mattress.

"Donny, I apologize in advance for this whooping I'm getting ready to give you," Marcel said, warning Rydon.

Unsure of what he got himself into, it was a good thing Rydon was great at method acting. No matter how he felt inside, he couldn't break character, having the reputation as the hardest rock in the garden.

"That's what I'm talking about!" Rydon shouted.

<pre>
            Vidor, Texas
          Boxer's Warehouse
      1:00PM Central Standard Time
      1959 December 23, Wednesday
</pre>

"I didn't know you still had it in you, Marcel. If you didn't slow down, why'd you retire?" Rydon asked.

"My heart wasn't in it anymore," Marcel replied, shrugging his shoulders. Closing the warehouse door shut, he shook his head daydreaming about his glory days.

"I know exactly what you mean. I was starting to feel the same way. Jo probably saved my career as a detective. You can ask Gabby, I was this close to retiring," Rydon said, pinching his fingers together.

"To do what!?" Marcel laughed. "I don't think you can do anything else but help people. Look at you now, the only reason you're here is to help Big Jo."

"You sound like Gab. How is the case going, Jo? You haven't said much about it since you first said something about it," Rydon said, still amped up from his sparring session.

"I don't like talking about it. We had the preliminary hearing about a month ago and they're pressing charges. The trial begins January 15th."

"That's the same day as Doc's birthday dinner," Rydon replied.

"Can you believe it? I most definitely planned on being in Atlanta that weekend," Jo replied. "I might still be able to make it."

"Don't worry about it, brother, it's all part of the Big Man's plan."

"Wise words."

Minutes after easily his most demanding practice of the year, a loud screeching noise interrupted the men as they conversed about the rest of their days in Vidor.

Speeding down the street, a white truck made a U-turn and screeched to a halt next to Jo's car. "GO BACK UP NORTH!" a man shouted, standing up on the flatbed of the truck as he launched a huge chunk of brick.

CRASH!

The brick smashed into the front windshield of Jo's rented Pentagon Bliss; the men fled as quickly as they arrived. "THAT'LL BE YOUR FACE IF WE CATCH YOU OUT AFTER DARK! NO BLACKS AFTER DARK!" The driver yelled shaking his fist out the window.

Chasing after the bandits on foot, Rydon stopped at the corner realizing it was a lost cause. "We can't even train in peace!?" he shouted angrily. "They must've been watching us this whole time. You know Jefferson sent them, right?" Rydon asked, pointing his first two fingers at Marcel and Jo.

"I just got this car," Jo said with his head hung. Brushing the glass off the seat, he leaned in to collect his belongings from the inside. "Can I ride in the limo with the Champ?"

"Whenever it arrives. Bentley should've been here by now," Rydon answered.

Lost in the middle of nowhere without a ride or means to communicate, the men were getting weary. Rydon buzzed the Direction Box for his driver several times to no avail and he was beginning to wonder. "You don't think they took Bentley, do you?"

"I hope not," Marcel answered, not knowing the truth himself.

Just as Marcel answered the question, the front end of a 1960 Pentagon Enchantment stretch limousine rounded the corner. "Sorry I'm late, sir. I couldn't find you. The Direction Box worked perfectly fine until I was about a mile out. Then it started making sounds and shorting out."

"No excuses, Bentley. There's a map in the glove box," Rydon replied.

"Yes, sir," he answered, closing the backseat door behind them.

"Is that what it was doing?" Rydon asked from the back seat, pointing to a flickering screen.

"Yes, but only within a mile or so. When you first buzzed the box, it worked perfectly fine."

As the driver reached the Black House Suites of Rose City, Rydon exited the limousine on his own accord, storming off toward the glass doors. "Don't take it personal," Jo reassured the driver who was certain he made his last drop off for the company.

Following in after the Number One Contender, Jo and Marcel jogged up the east stairwell calling his name. "Donny!?"

"Don!?" they yelled.

Knowing the type of person Rydon was, both men already knew his next move. Unable to slow his progress, they were able to catch the door to his penthouse suite just before it closed shut. To no one's surprise, he was on the phone dialing numbers.

"Eight o'clock sharp," he said, slamming the phone down on the hook. "Y'all seem mighty calm about this," Rydon barked.

Rydon was big on principle. *An eye for an eye* must have been written specifically with him in mind. He was a master of peace but was also the King of Justice. He never took things lightly and as a result, he lost many hours of sleep at night making wrong things, right.

As time passed, Rydon became more and more restless. Once his engine was revved there was no stopping him until his mission was complete. The closer it got to eight o'clock, the more people arrived at the conference room of the penthouse suite.

"The meeting will come to order on Wednesday, December 23, 1959. 8:00PM, room 2208 of the Rose City, Black House Suites. All rise, for the pledge."

I pledge to Secret Seven, the number of completion.
Helping advance the world's people is our only mission.
Getting rid of bigots, teaching them history.
If they try to harm me, may the Big Man be with them.

"You all know why I brought you here," Rydon announced to the group, beginning the meeting. "Folks of Vidor passed an underground ordinance that forbids black folks from being outside after dark. They say this is a *sundown town.* As you all know, I have a fight in a few nights and if they were bold enough to throw a brick through my promoter's window earlier today, imagine what they would do to other folks.

"I brought you in early because we have to be tighter than ever when our families, friends, and supporters, touchdown."

Rydon circled the room, rallying his troops. "Don't think for one second because the cameras are rolling, they won't do something wild," he said, pausing before lifting his arms as he continued.

"They control the media!" Rydon shouted. "Now, we have five thousand people coming from the city to watch this fight. It's fifty of you all here right now and all of you have a hundred soldiers a piece!" Rydon exclaimed.

"Keep the people safe and folks from Vidor too. Let me know right now if you need more manpower because I don't want to hear any excuses if someone gets hurt. You dig?" Rydon said calmly, seeking confirmation.

"Yes, sir!" the room rumbled.

"Come on now. Say it like you mean it, Lieutenants!" Rydon demanded.

"YES, SIR!"

Rose City, Texas
Black House Suites
4:00PM Central Standard Time
1959 December 26, Saturday

All packed up and ready for the biggest day of his professional boxing career, Rydon refused to leave the room without his good luck kisses. "Gab, I'm on my way out," he announced through the door of the master bathroom.

"Ok, give me two seconds."

"One, two, now you owe me double." Rydon chuckled.

Opening the door, ready for the day. Gabriella kissed her husband goodbye. "One, two, bye. Good luck, see you tonight. I'll be wearing lavender, front row, seat fifty-eight, west wall.

"I'll find you," he said, locking the door behind him as he headed to the main lobby.

"Greetings, sir," Bentley said, taking Rydon's bags before opening his door.

"Good afternoon, Bentley."

Before their departure, Bentley made an announcement through the vehicle's speaker system. "Excuse me, sir," he called. "I talked to old man Grove about what happened with the Direction Box. Do you have it with you?"

"What did he say?" Rydon asked, removing the device from his backpack.

"He said that only happens if its running at the same frequency as something else with a higher or matching frequency, which is very rare. Press the button again, will you?"

Moving the Direction Box closer to the front of the limousine, Rydon pressed the button and the driver's Direction Box unit went haywire. Displaying arrows in every direction. "Now what?" he asked.

"Well, he said that it has to be something on you since it doesn't happen with any of our other clients. Do you have any tracking devices or transmitters?"

"Not on me. I'm on vacation," Rydon answered.

"Here, sir, he gave me this," Bentley said, handing Rydon a glowing wand, showing him how to start the scan.

Waving the light across his body, he was clear without a sound. Holding the wand over his backpack, it started to vibrate. By the time he got to the bottom of the bag, the vibration grew stronger.

Reaching into the bag he pulled out the black sweatpants responsible for triggering the alarm. Removing the silver watch he received from George, Rydon found the source. "I should have known," he said, shaking his head. "I got too comfortable."

A tool kit in the front pocket of the bag he carried had what he needed to finish the job. Popping open the case, he removed a small chip with a blinking red light. "Lived Industrial," Rydon read aloud. "Ever heard of them before?"

"Can't say that I have," Bentley answered.

"They supplied weapons for the Watcherz during the Civil War." Removing the chip from the timepiece, Rydon asked for a favor. "Do you have a small bag up there?"

"No. But, I have this," Bentley said removing the lid to his empty fruit cup, drying the pineapple juice residue left behind.

"Thank you, tell old man Grove he's my hero," Rydon said, laughing at his pain as he placed the chip inside the fruit cup. "How did I miss that?" he whispered aloud, shaking his head as he relaxed in his seat.

```
              Vidor, Texas
    Kurt Kamen Kaine's House of Pain
       8:00PM Central Standard Time
       1959 December 26, Saturday
```

With less than an hour to spare before the title bout, Rydon sat alone in the locker room with just his thoughts during the last undercard fight.

This is it big man, he can't stop me.
Don't forget about the brick.
He turned George against me.
That's too many reasons to whoop this man already.
He doesn't have a chance.
I'm the Champ...

Walking with a prideful stride to the ring, the beat of African drums and brass trumpets preceded Rydon's presence. It was obvious Rydon wasn't the same fighter he was the first time he faced the Journeyman. He had attitude, swagger, and a will to win that seemed unbreakable.

Entering the four corners, boos and obscenities filled the ring like a flooded Wayne County freeway. Five thousand cheers were drowned out by forty thousand jeers. Rydon was everyone's emotional rock. Most thought he was a bit cold-hearted because they never saw him rattled.

Suddenly, for the first time in his documented history, Rydon's look was one of doubt. He had no control of his situation and all he could think of was the safety of his wife and guests from the Brother Cities.

Looking for the lavender dress by the west wall, he bowed down to Queen Gabriella in front of millions at home and just under fifty thousand in attendance. Waving with a smile, paparazzi were the first to pop the bulbs of their flashes for a shot of Mrs. Powers-Tyme, 1959 LOTT Woman of the Year.

The sound of breaking glass and smashed bricks meant Delaware Jefferson was up next.

Making his way to the ring, former heavyweight champion of the world and current Top Challenger, Delaware Journeyman... Jefferson!

Screams from ringside to the upper deck made it obvious who the fan favorite was. In the best shape of his life with a much easier demeanor, the Journeyman jogged down the aisle and dove into the ring. He held his hand behind his ear as he slid on his stomach. Asking the crowd for more, they went berserk.

Even Rydon seemed impressed by the Journeyman's showmanship. It was like facing a cloned, exaggerated version of himself.

The meeting in the center of the ring had the Mighty Mouth rather silent. Standing with no telling sign of emotion, the referee went on with the pre-fight rituals. "I know you two know the rules because we discussed them less than an hour ago. I don't want any surprises in my square. Let's make history the right way men, touch gloves," the referee concluded.

Smiling at a docile Rydon the whole time, the Journeyman seemed to have turned the tables early on. Taking a seat on the stool for his final instruction before the bell, Rydon tuned out his trainers to focus on his inner thoughts.

He's studied my moves and mastered my style.
Sticking to the game plan will get me DROPPED!
Remember the brick...
Where's Gab?

Looking over to his wife, he gave her a wink, reminding her everything would be ok.

Round One

Tyme and Jefferson are jogging toward each other, dancing in the center of the ring. This is mighty interesting don't you think? Folks, I'm here with the three time heavyweight champion, Ralph Ruh.

What's happening, people? It's Big Ruh and I'm here to tell you that Wilcox isn't a square like everyone thinks. This cat has style.

Thank you, Mr. Ruh, you look sharp yourself. Tyme versus Jefferson II. Who are you taking because this one may get interesting.

I know they say the student is always better than the teacher and looking at Delaware's last six or seven fights, he's definitely been studying Tyme's

117

style. The thing is you don't know Tyme like I know him. I'd bet you a million bucks he's over there recreating the wheel right now.

Why does everyone in Tyme's camp always say that? **You don't know Tyme like I know him.** *What does that mean, Mr. Ruh? We're begging.*

The man is a workaholic. Whatever he does, it's in his nature to be the best at it. Whether it's fighting crime, tracing family lineage, or boxing. I sparred with him not too long ago. He's the real deal, people.

Well, there you have it. Every time I try bringing someone neutral to the table, they're an advocate for the Chosen Dreamer.

Not necessarily an advocate, we just recognize greatness when we see it. I fought the Journeyman three times, and the last time wasn't too long ago. I sparred with Tyme a couple months ago and like I said, he's the real deal.

There you have it once again. I won't press the issue. In the ring the two are still feeling each other out. Almost the exact same way as the last time they fought. Whoa! Journeyman missed a Poster Punch that might've taken Tyme out of the game.

Did you see the look on Tyme's face as he dodged a move that he brought to the PBA? He's angry now.

Perhaps you're right, after that combination to the body by Tyme. Pushing off, he circles the ring before charging at the Journeyman with a right blow to the body and a right hook to the head! Ruh is right! He is angry.

Uh-oh, look at the Journeyman...

Taking another move from Tyme's playbook he zigs and zags backward, before lighting Tyme up with a blow to a chin made of steel. Tyme didn't budge. He's shaking his head 'no' as if he's unphased but that push to Jefferson shows his frustration; something we haven't seen from him in the past. Will his emotions help or hurt him? Ruh, what do you think?

I think it could go either way.

In another tango around the ring, the two have only thrown a combined thirty-seven punches, with one minute left in the first. Here we go! Every time I downplay the action, they make me look silly.

You make yourself look silly, Scott.

Thank you, Mr. Ruh. Journeyman throws a nice jab and right hand uppercut that forces Tyme to push off again. Tyme looks like he's finally met his match. The blueprint he's been laying for up-and-coming fighters may have hurt him today.

I've never seen him get hit with so many clean punches in one round before. Great accuracy by the Journeyman.

Ding! Ding!

You don't say. The Referee is on it, separating the two as the bell sounds.

Round Two

And we're back to start the second round. The judges gave the round to the Journeyman.

The Steel Chin doesn't seem too concerned. He can't take his eyes off the lady in the front row. Looks like that's where the real fight is! Mrs. Powers-Tyme just dumped a cup of water on that old man. Woah and a bucket of popcorn!

Security is taking her out of here pretty quickly. They were taking her out... Now some other men have stepped in to escort her out of the arena the way a lady should while the Steel Chin stares on from the ring. I don't think he's blinked yet.

That's Secret Seven.

Secret Seven?

They're everywhere. This one won't last much longer after that.

I might have to agree with you.

Ding! Ding!

Tyme is storming like a cloudy sky as the Journeyman jabs and moves. I don't know if his hand speed is a problem for Tyme or if he's just proving a point. I've learned you never know with this guy. The most unpredictable fighter I've ever covered.

Second that.

Tyme's taking all the Journeyman's got to give. Losing so much weight must have taken away his power.

I don't know about that. Tyme's left eye looks swollen.

Yes, it does. The right one too. A push off by Tyme sends the Journeyman back to the center of the ring.

Uh-oh...

Uh-oh is right! Boing! What a Poster Punch by the Originator. He's not stopping there, folks. He's been lighting up Journeyman Jefferson's face for about five seconds, real time.

Journeyman thinks he has something to prove, trying to eat Tyme's punches. That's a terrible strategy against this man. His punches carry venom. They sting after the bite.

Well put. Tyme's not in a dancing mood, he's got Jefferson backed into the corner. What a sight to see folks. He's beating up on the Journeyman badly. Tyme's not a tall man. He's about six feet, but he's beating up this 6'5 man like the kid who has had enough of the school bully.

Well put. You have me laughing on radio. They're never going to ask me back. Thanks a lot, Scott.

Sure, they will. There it is! The first knock down of the night. That was more like a drop down don't you think? Journeyman couldn't take the punches and just dropped to his bottom. Like a big ole baby. Now I'm laughing. See, I do it all the time. It's good for the soul.

"1... 2... 3... 4... 5... 6... 7... 8... Are you ready?" Referee Armstrong asked as Delaware Jefferson nodded his head, yes.

Journeyman is back to his feet after a standing eight count. Tyme is picking up where he left off with a hook to the body. Journeyman couldn't move after that blow. That punch set up a massive right cross by Tyme. I don't think he's missed a punch all round.

This one is getting ugly.

Journeyman must feel the same as he takes another knee! Too much venom in those punches, I'd guess. Now you got me thinking of new nicknames.

Here we go again.

Hear me out. What about Scorpion?

No

Stingray?

Nope

The Wasp

Sounds like a superhero.

Viper, Lionfish, Gila Monster!

That's it, Viper.

Viper it is! Another striking blow by the Viper! He smells fear folks. The Journeyman's pride is the only thing keeping him on his feet at this point. This fight may be over soon.

Looks like he's getting ready to take another knee.

Not if the Viper can help it. He's picking him up, by the underarms but the Journeyman is dropping his weight anyway. I've never seen anything like it. Ralph Ruh is laughing tears right now folks.

"1... 2... 3... 4... 5... 6... 7... 8... You do something like that again, Jefferson and this fight is over. You hear me, are you ready?" the referee warned, as Delaware shook his head.

Here comes Tyme again. Throwing stingers to the body, arms, head, and anywhere else. I don't remember the last time Journeyman threw a punch. He's been on the defense for so long. I think he's lost. I bet you anything, he doesn't know where he is right now.

No one watching this fight would take that bet.

Here comes a Poster Punch, Ouch! A zig-zag slam and a blast to the solar plexus by the Viper! Journeyman is going down folks. That blow to the body just saw to it!

"1... 2... 3... 4... 5... 6... 7... 8... 9... 10! You're out!"

That's it! We have a new heavyweight champion right here in Vidor, Texas! It's the Chosen Dreamer! Would you look at that belt. Leather and gold never looked so good together. Do you hear the fans? This could get out of hand in a hurry.

"Boo!!!"
"Get out of Texas!"
"You know what happens after dark!"
"There's no way out, boy!"

Let's act like grownups people. The man won the fight fair and square. I've never seen a champion so alert after a fight. You don't think anything will happen, do you, Ruh? Ruh?

Ralph Ruh has left to help police the situation in the ring. It all started when the Journeyman went over to shake Tyme's hand. He didn't do so quietly and the two almost came to blows without gloves which is what caused people in the stands to rush the ring.

What they didn't know was, Tyme didn't come alone. They just took thirty to forty people out of here.

It is sad folks have to be forced to behave sometimes. There must be hundreds of those Secret Seven agents that Ruh was telling us about. Now that we have some order in here, we go to the ring with the Champ who's live with Cynthia Holmes.

"Ten wins, all by knockout, no losses. You're the Professional Boxing Association's quickest champion. It's been less than a year since you signed your contract. No one in PBA history has won the crown so soon. Tell us, how did you do it?"

"Hard work and belief. We work hard *every* day," Rydon said, holding up ones on both hands. Pausing to celebrate with the fans and his new belt. "Once they convinced me to come back to boxing, I knew this day would come. It was only a matter of time. To my trainer Marcel Riaz, thank you!" Rydon shouted as the fans let out a thunderous applause for the retired champion turned trainer.

"He's the only person who's ever knocked me down. He did it when we were seven." Rydon laughed.

"I figured I'd tell you before he did. My Promoter, Jo Rivers is the best in the business! And to my wife, who one of you cowards ran off, I love you. One more continent left on the list baby, we're going to Africa!"

"Boo!!!"

Here come the boo birds again. I wish they would just be quiet.

"Early on, you looked intimidated. Did you have any doubt?" Holmes asked.

"I was never doubtful. I just know where we are and got worried about my wife. I'm kind of glad she got thrown out. It gave me some peace of mind."

"What do you mean by *where we are?*"

"We're in a place where they threaten black folks' lives if you're caught outside after dark. A place where they throw bricks through windshields in daylight to remind you about it. A place where my wife had to throw her popcorn at a man for who knows why. And a place where you have to bring your own security, to make sure folks act right. *That's* what I mean by *where we are.*"

"Well, alright. Your new heavyweight champion... Rydon Tyme!" she announced, holding his arm high to the sky.

Five thousand Michiganders and citizens of Vidor were escorted outside the arena and onto the Big Buses awaiting them outside. "Coach!" Rydon shouted, weaving through the crowd on his way out of the ring.

"What's up, Champ!? Congratulations." Marcel exclaimed, pounding fists.

"Thanks, Coach. I couldn't have done it without you."

"Anytime, it was an honor having you in the gym again."

"It was great being back. Can you do me a favor?" Rydon requested.

"What's up, Champ?"

"Have Bentley take you back to the *training facility*. If that's what you want to call it and drop off their equipment at eleven o'clock."

"I thought you were going to show the PBA how bad it was?" Marcel replied with confusion.

"I was but I have something better in mind. After you get there, just throw the bag out the window and keep moving."

"Deal," Marcel agreed.

"I'll see y'all back at the suite around midnight. You heard anything about Gab?" Rydon asked, wiping the sweat from his eyebrow.

"She's in the locker room waiting area. Right next to where the photo shoot is with the families and Young Champ. We had them escorted to the back immediately after the KO," Marcel replied as they parted ways.

Going along with the plan, Marcel did just as he was instructed. No more than fifteen minutes later, a pack of trucks and motorcycles pulled up to the warehouse.

"You said he'd be here. Well, where is he, George?" One of the men asked, spitting to the dirt road.

"He should be, this says he's right here," George said, holding a device similar to the Direction Box, as a voice called from up above.

"I am," Rydon said, climbing down from the roof of the warehouse. "At least you know it works," he continued as seven Pentagon Colts blocked every escape route. Twenty Secret Seven soldiers came from behind the shadows and surrounded the men, forcing them into the warehouse.

"You boys rest peacefully now," Rydon spoke to the bunch, locking the warehouse door and gate from the outside.

"You won't get away with this!" one man shouted as the door shut.

```
                    Amarna, Egypt
                     8:13PM GMT
              1960 February 21, Sunday
```

February 12, 1960

To: THE Heavyweight Champion of the World!

I want to start by saying, thank you. If it weren't for you, I think, check that, I know I would have gotten a much harsher sentence. 30 days in the county jail and 6 months probation is a lot more manageable than the 10 years I was facing.

When you looked the judge in his eyes on that witness stand and said, "Your honor, as a practicing attorney at law, I know the judicial system was put in place to rehabilitate criminals. Mr. Rivers isn't a criminal, he's an entrepreneur. I haven't seen any evidence presented that was collected within the last 10 years. But what we have seen is all the hard work he put in turning a small city detective into an international sensation."

You gave me creditability alright. Your testimony made the judge view me in a different light. Until your name was called, I don't think he looked at me once. But when you started speaking, I saw empathy in his eyes.

"Mr. Rivers is a product of his environment who found a way out. In his escape, he brought me with him. I haven't been happy at work in years but because of him, I can't wait to get

back to the office. Without a doubt, he's the best in the business." I don't want to fill this letter with quotes, you know what you said. I just wanted you to know you are appreciated.

24 days left! When I get out of here, let me know if you need anything. I owe you 6 months of community service. I'd love to visit schools with you to talk to the kids. I've decided to dedicate the rest of my days keeping them off the streets and out of trouble.

Thanks for everything,
Joab Rivers

P.S. Look... I know you're newly retired, I know this. But keep in mind you still have a Boxer's Option on the table. If you want to defend the belts or go after being undisputed, that'd be HUGE! And you know what they say. The early birds win championships... Think about it.

Rydon Tyme: The Life of the Eye
The Case of the Stolen Silver
(2 of 5)

Preview

Ricki's Ruby Jewelry and Loans
Highland Park, Michigan
15700 Woodward Avenue
10:12PM Eastern Standard Time
1951 April 12

As most autumn nights, the streets of Highland Park were at ease like a well negotiated peace treaty. Storefronts and sidewalks had been barren for hours. The only sounds belonged to the tires coming to a halt across the smooth, wet pavement of Woodward Avenue.

Breaking the silence was an exhausted Beverly Tyler, exiting Ricki's Ruby, a Highland Park jewelry store. Scurrying off into the night she dodged the rain pellets above her. Climbing into the back seat of a taxi that awaited her on the corner of Woodward Avenue, she vanished into the night.

Noon arrived like clockwork, never late or absent. Through rain, snow, sleet, and hail, one could always count on Father Time's arrival. After a good night's sleep and a hearty meal, it was back to the place she departed not long ago.

Beverly returned to a completely different work environment that April afternoon. As the last person scheduled to report for work, she was also last to hear about the big news.

Walking over to her friend and coworker Decia Delgado, Beverley attempted to figure out what was going on. "Why is everyone so stiff today?" she asked.

"They're going to tell you any minute now. They advised us not to speak until everyone has been questioned." Decia answered quickly, trying not to carry on a lengthy conversation.

"They? They who? And what do you mean questioned? What happened?" Beverly asked, searching for answers.

"You'll see and yes questioned. Something big happened last night. That's all I can say," Decia said, dusting the glass display case.

Along her way to the break room, Beverly stopped in front of a mirror at the end of the hallway to fix her wool, fuchsia colored scarf.

She entered the employee breakroom, placing her timesheet in the payroll bin. As she turned to make her way to the sales floor, she was startled by a stranger.

"Are you Beverly Tyler?" the man asked.

"Who wants to know?" Beverly replied.

"Me, are you?" the stranger asked a second time.

"You shouldn't walk up on folks like that, sir. You're going to give someone a heart attack one of these days. Yes, I'm Beverly Tyler. How can I help you?"

"You have to be more aware of your surroundings, Miss Tyler. I've been sitting here since you walked in. Come with me."

Beverly followed the man, dressed in black down the dim hallways of the jewelry store. The big, framed sunglasses he sported indoors led her to believe that his eyes were sensitive to the halogen lights in the breakroom.

"Have a seat please," the man said, motioning to an empty seat.

"Sure," Beverly said in a low tone.

2

"What do you know about last night's inventory, anything strange?" he asked.

"Besides the fact that I came in on my off day, I was really tired when I got home."

"What do you mean *off day*?" he wondered, adjusting his eyewear.

"I was scheduled the day off, but Ricki and Lara asked me to help with the inventory. I could use the extra money, so I said, yes." Beverly shrugged, still unaware of what was going on.

"Ma'am, did anything else seem strange or odd?"

"It took a lot longer that's for sure. We had two more counts than usual," she said, after taking some time.

"Why do you think that might have happened?"

"Normally after the first and second counts, we get a list of missing big ticket items."

"What's considered a big ticket item?"

"Big ticket items are priced between fifty and one hundred dollars. Anything over one hundred dollars is considered a major purchase. Management counts major purchases."

"What happens after you get the list, ma'am? This isn't telling me much," the man said, sitting his pen down on the wooden table.

"Ricki, Ruby, and Lara were the only ones who saw the numbers after the second count. I don't know what else to tell you, sir."

"Last night, you counted three extra times?" he asked, reaching for his pen to jot down notes on a yellow legal pad, nestled inside a leather portfolio.

"No, twice," Beverly assured him.

4

"Typically, what happens during a recount?" he queried.

"We check display cases, mannequins, desks, drawers, underneath the register. Basically, places we might hide if we were missing rings or bracelets."

"Does management ever report losses and gains to the staff after an inventory?"

"I'm sorry, I've already said way too much. I don't even know who you are," Beverly announced with her head tilted.

Rydon Tyme: The Life of the Eye
The Case of the Stolen Silver (2 of 5)

ABOUT THE AUTHOR

Ali Muhammad was born and raised in Highland Park, Michigan. After graduating from Western Michigan University with a Bachelor of Science degree in Professional Education, Muhammad began his Teaching career in one of West Michigan's Title I public schools.

In 2015, Muhammad pursued a second career in writing and has five published works to date. Debut novel, *Michigan International University*. Children's book, *Wake Up Little Lion*. *Nobody Cares, Bad Move,* and *Prize Fighter* from the *Rydon Tyme: Life of the Eye* series.

During production for LOTT Magazine (2018), Muhammad was promoted from Lead Writer to Editor-In-Chief. In 2020, he fulfilled a five-project production deal. Prize Fighter is the first installment of a new three-project deal Muhammad signed with Leaders of Tomorrow, Today LLC in 2021.

www.LOTT48203.COM

Books by the Author:

Michigan International University (2015)   Wake Up Little Lion (2016)

Nobody Cares (2019)   Bad Move (2020)   Prize Fighter (2022)

www.LOTT48203.COM

www.ingramcontent.com/pod-product-compliance
Lightning Source LLC
Chambersburg PA
CBHW071924220626
47052CB00002B/442